GHETTO
COWBOY

GHETTO

COWBOY

a novel by
G. NERI

illustrated by
JESSE JOSHUA WATSON

CANDLEWICK PRESS

Text copyright © 2011 by G. Neri
Illustrations copyright © 2011 by Jesse Joshua Watson

First paperback edition 2013

The Library of Congress has cataloged the hardcover edition as follows:

Neri, Greg.
Ghetto cowboy / G. Neri ; illustrated by Jesse Joshua Watson. — 1st ed.
p. cm.
Summary: Twelve-year-old Cole's behavior causes his mother to drive him from
Detroit to Philadelphia to live with a father he has never known, but who soon
has Cole involved with a group of African-American "cowboys" who rescue
horses and use them to steer youths away from drugs and gangs.
ISBN 978-0-7636-4922-7 (hardcover)
[1. Fathers and sons—Fiction. 2. Horses—Fiction.
3. City and town life—Pennsylvania—Fiction. 4. Conduct of life—Fiction.
5. Moving, Household—Fiction. 6. African Americans—Fiction.
7. Philadelphia (Pa.)—Fiction.] I. Watson, Jesse Joshua, ill. II. Title.
PZ7.N4377478Ghe 2011
[Fic]—dc22   2010007565

ISBN 978-0-7636-6453-4 (paperback)

21 22 23 24 TRC 16 15 14 13

Printed in Eagan, MN, U.S.A.

This book was typeset in Century Schoolbook.
The illustrations were done in pencil, ink, and acrylic
on illustration board, processed digitally.

Candlewick Press
99 Dover Street
Somerville, Massachusetts 02144

visit us at www.candlewick.com

For my dad
G. N.

For Greg and Edward, my boys. And to the youth
in the ghetto: rise up and ride on!
J. J. W.

ONE

We drivin' into the sunset, the car burning up from the heat. I don't know if it's comin' from outside or from Mama, who's burning up angry at me. She ain't said nothin' to me since we left the principal's office 'bout a hour ago. But she got her foot pressed on the gas like we in a race, zoomin' past everyone on the expressway.

"I can't do this no more, Cole."

"Do what?" I say.

But I know. I only seen her this angry once before, and this is worse.

"Where we going?" I ask.

She don't answer. By the time we hit the interstate outta Detroit, I can see she crying. I hate when she do that. It makes me feel bad inside, 'cause I'm always the one who makes her feel that way.

"I'm sorry, Mama."

She wipes her eyes on her sleeve.

"Me too, baby. Me too," she says, all sad.

I see the city slowly disappearing, turning into suburbs. I know she gotta work early in the morning, so we can't be driving that far. I ask her again.

"Where we going?"

Cars is falling behind us 'cause she speedin' *up*.

"Mama—"

She chokes it out: "Philadelphia."

I laugh, then see she ain't joking.

"*What?!*" I stare at her hard.

Her hands is shaking, so she grab the steering wheel tighter.

"*Philly?*" I say, my head spinning. "What for?"

She pulls on her hair and grunts. "I can't be your mama right now. You need a man in your life."

I try to let that sink in, but my ears is on fire. "What you talking about? Who's in Philly?"

She sighs.

"Your daddy."

2

My daddy.

Who I never met.

Who Mama never talks about.

Once I asked if she had a picture of him, and she said she burned 'em all. When I kept on her, all she said was he didn't care about us and now he gone and good riddance.

She never said nothing more.

Now I find out we gonna go see him?

"Why?"

She just holds up her hand like she can't even go there, like the idea that she gonna take me to him is the last thing she'd ever do.

But she doing it. And then it hits me: "You wanna get rid of me."

That gets her. I can see her holding that steering wheel so tight her knuckles is turning white. "I can't do this no more," she says to no one. "After twelve years, I got nothing left."

That's crazy talk. She can't leave me. "But you my mama! *You* supposed to watch out for me!"

She bites her lip, her eyes locked on some faraway place. "I used to think your daddy was a bad father . . . that he didn't know how to take care of us. But now I'm thinking there's something wrong with me 'cause I don't know why you are the way you are,"

3

she say. "Maybe he's the only one left who can turn you around."

She startin' to scare me now, talkin' like that. "I ain't so bad, Mama. I can do better."

She nod, fightin' for words. "I know you can, baby. You just need someone that can show you the way. But that ain't me no more, Cole."

I can't believe what I'm hearin'. "So you gonna leave me with some dude who never cared about us? Some guy who treated you so bad, you never talk about him?"

She stares ahead, her eyes wet. She ain't disagreeing. "He's different is all. But maybe different is what you need."

And with that, she just shuts down.

I seen that look before. It means she made up her mind. I think about grabbing that steering wheel and turning the car around, but she like a rock and, deep down, I know I gone too far this time.

TWO

I stare out the window. Even though it's getting dark out, I can see we in the middle a nowhere. No lights from no city.

Nothing. It looks just like I feel, all empty inside.

I don't know why I stopped going to school. I guess I didn't wanna waste no more time with teachers and homework and all a that, 'cause what difference do it make in the end? I'll never do nothing great in my life. Do they really think I'm gonna be like Obama? Not a chance. I just feel sorry for Mama for thinking that I could be somebody.

She just found out yesterday that I missed the last four weeks of school. That I been hiding them letters and erasing the messages from the vice principal, even duckin' the truancy officer when he comes by.

With her working so much, that wasn't so hard to do 'cause I done it before and knew all the tricks. But it was the first time I got caught, on account of the truancy officer finding me tagging the back of the school cafeteria while school was going on. Stupid.

She really lost it when she found out they was gonna suspend me for the rest of the year. If I wasn't twelve, they woulda kicked me out for good, but now they talking about holding me back.

I ain't never seen her so sad before, like she thought it was all her fault. It made me feel like dirt seeing her sittin' on the kitchen floor crying, but I knew there was nothin' I could do to help her, 'cept to let her get it all out. That's how we deal.

Today, Mama had to skip work to come in to talk to the principal. He went on and on about how I was in danger—rattling off a buncha numbers like how four outta every ten black boys drop outta school, and seven outta ten can't get no job and 'cause a that, six of us will end up in prison. I could see Mama sinking into herself, like he was saying it was all her fault for not being a good mama.

In the old days, seemed she had the energy to read to me and stuff, and we made drawings together or laid under the covers, talking about where we would go if we could live anywhere else but Detroit. . . .

But that was when I was a kid. Them days is gone. Kids can be happy 'cause they don't know better, but when you get older, well, you just know it's all a big lie. Last three years, Mama's been so moody, like a cloud passed in front of her face. Sometime she look at me and it's like she don't see me. I been on my own a lot 'cause a that and 'cause she gotta work so much. I been roaming the streets, skippin' school and hanging with my friends, staying out late, which she don't like. We ain't been doing nothing bad . . . but we ain't exactly been doin' nothing good neither.

It was weird hearing the principal say things about me like I wasn't there, even though I was. He told Mama that since there was a couple weeks left of school, he was gonna suspend me till the summer session started. He said that going to summer school was the only way I could get outta repeating the seventh grade, and not only did I have to show up, but I had to pass the end-of-year exam too. Then he said I needed to seriously think about my life so I could get my priorities straight. Otherwise, things was gonna get much worse for me, and I would end up like one of them boys he was talkin' about.

Looking at Mama's face, I could tell she already thought it was too late.

THREE

We drive for hours, Mama's eyes red from crying and being all tired out. When we finally stop for gas, she goes to a phone booth and makes a call.

I can't hear what she saying, but there's a fight going on. Her hands is all over the place, banging on the glass, pulling on her hair, biting her nails. Finally, she hangs up and just stands there, staring at the phone.

When she comes back to the car, I know I gotta say something.

"I can be better, Mama. I won't skip school no more. I promise."

She looks at me for the first time, her eyes searchin' mine. It's like she wanna remember my face. Her mouth is tight, but she takes my hand, shaking her head slowly. I know she wanna say something, but it feels like if she opens her mouth, she just gonna crumble apart like them old auto factories near our apartment.

Finally, she starts up the car.

I ask one last time. "Can we go home?"

She takes a deep breath and exhales slowly. "No. Don't ask me again."

"But what about school? How'm I gonna do summer school if I ain't there?"

She shakes her head. "That's up to your daddy now."

We drive all night, stopping only at a drive-through and a coupla rest stops. I don't know how she can drive so much. I'm going crazy just sittin' here. I keep waiting for her to stop and turn around, but she don't.

Next thing I know, I see the sun coming up. It hurts my eyes. Did she drive through the night?

Mama stops the car, and my eyes focus in the side mirror. I can see we in the city somewhere, on some run-down street.

Is this Philly? I musta fallen asleep just watching them cars go by and listening to Mama's old Mariah Carey CDs. My face is sitting in drool on the windowsill.

Suddenly, something big and white bumps up against the car, and I jump. I think I must be dreamin', 'cause I just saw a horse run by.

I spin around just in time to see something disappear around the corner. Then I see a dazed old woman in a bathrobe walk past us. About five or six guys come running out of a house half-dressed, and disappear around the corner too.

What's going on?

Mama pays no mind. She staring at a building across the street.

This is definitely the 'hood. The buildings is all row houses cramped together, made of old brick and dark windows that feel like they watching us. The place is crumbling apart—overgrown vacant lots stand empty between buildings, some boarded up, some barely holdin' on.

"Wait here," Mama says.

She gets out and walks up the stoop to the place she was staring at. Stands there awhile, then knocks. No one answers.

She knocks again, louder.

Finally someone opens the door. It's dark inside, so I can't see who it is. She goes in, the door closing behind her.

Where she going?

I get outta the car and think about going after her. Then I notice something move behind me. A coupla sleepy-eyed gangbangers have come outta one of the buildings, looking around.

The tall skinny one sees me and elbows his friend, who's built like a bull. They both older, maybe eighteen or something. They stare at me, and I get back into the car. Maybe they seen I was wearing my Pistons jersey. Dag. I know Philly is no fan of the Pistons.

When I see them coming over, I slouch down. They don't look happy, checking out the car like it's some alien spaceship that just landed on their block. They looking at the plates that shows we not from here.

Mama comes outta the house. She looks dead, like a zombie moving toward me. But that don't stop the guys behind us making comments, like how she so fine and all a that.

She ignores them, opens the trunk, and starts grabbing some big trash bags full of stuff.

"What you doing?" I say through the window.

She drags a few bags across the way and dumps them on the stoop. One of 'em tears open, and I see it's full of *my* stuff!

"Mama?"

She come back, grabs two more bags.

I jump outta the car. "Mama, what's going on—?"

The guys behind me is making fun, crying, *Mama, Mama.*

I run after her and grab her arm. "What you *doin'*?"

She drops the bags, stares at the ground. "You're staying here with your daddy."

My heart stops.

"You really gonna leave me?"

She starts back to the car.

I hold on. "You can't leave me here."

She stares at the ground. "You stay with your daddy. I can't help you no more."

"But Mama!" I cry out.

The guys laugh at me. "Mommy, Mommy!" I wanna kill 'em, but I don't have time.

She gets in the car and closes the door.

I bang on the window. "You can't leave me!"

She looks at me, tears in her eyes. She says something all quiet, but I can't hear what she talking about.

Then, in the reflection of the car window, I see a man behind me on the stoop.

I swing around and see a dude dressed—well, he looks like a cowboy.

Got a big ol' white cowboy hat, western shirt, big gold belt buckle, and cowboy boots. He looks like a cowboy except for the gray dreads coming down to his shoulders and the fact that he as black as me.

He picking up the bags and starting back into the house.

"Hey!" I yell, running over.

He looks at me kinda funny.

Then it hits me. "You my . . . daddy?" I ask.

He laughs, I guess 'cause he too old for that. "Not me, boy. They call me Jamaica Bob, on account of the dreads. I work with your daddy."

I take the bags from his hand. "I ain't staying."

I hear the car start up and swing around. "Mama!"

She looks at me scared. She mouths—*I'm sorry.*

Then it's like everything happens all at once.

A horse—that big white horse I thought I saw before—jumps out from around the corner just as Mama's car takes off. She looking back at me and don't see this monster coming.

There's a bunch of guys chasing the horse, and they see what's gonna happen before Mama or the horse can—

BOOM!

Mama's car sideswipes the horse. It hits the front of the car and the hood, then tumbles like a ton of bricks.

I can feel it hit the ground, and it's a awful sound—flesh and bone and metal all crunching together with the smell of burned rubber.

"Mama!"

I run toward the car. Mama looks in shock at the blood on the hood of her car. Her hands is shaking.

The horse is lying on its side, foaming at the mouth, its hoofs scraping at the brick street, trying to get up. All the guys is frozen like someone took a picture of 'em, their jaws hanging open.

I try to open the car door, but it's stuck. I bang on the window. "Mama! You okay?"

The only sound I hear is that horse kicking and scraping as it rolls around in pain.

And that's when I see my daddy.

I can tell it's him 'cause as soon as I see him walk onto the street, it's like I'm lookin' into the future or something. He looks exactly like me, only taller and older. And he definitely ain't in a good mood.

I'm about to say something, but he just brushes past me.

Then I see the gun in his hand.

Holy—

I think he gonna go after Mama, but he stops in front of her window, and when she forces the door open, he just pushes it back closed and points her away, like she done enough damage for one day.

Her eyes is red with tears, like her heart been ripped in two. She tries the key and pumps the gas until the engine chokes to life. The car backs out slowly, her bumper half off and grating on the street, leaving a small trail of sparks. She stops when she knocks into some trash cans. It feels like she can't do nothing right today.

Mama stares at me, like maybe this'll be the last time I'll ever see her. Then she turns down a alley and is gone.

I look at the skid marks on the empty street and feel everyone behind me staring at my back. I hear that horse gasping for breath, and it feels like me — like I had all the wind sucked right outta me. I can't breathe.

The horse moans and groans, getting louder and louder until I hear the cock of the gun and a loud *BANG!*

Then it's quiet again.

FOUR

It seem like a year passes before someone says something.

"Where Mrs. Elders at?"

Someone else says, "I saw her wandering. I told her to fix that gate, but no. Now look."

Jamaica Bob butts in. "That's a shame, man. This one coulda been one righteous horse if Mr. Elders was still here, bless his soul. Can't blame a widow for this mess."

Then the man I think is my daddy says, "Better get it off the street before the City hears about it."

"But Harp, it ain't our business."

"Ain't our business? You know anything that goes down on Chester Avenue, they'll be blaming us. We can't give 'em any reason to close us down."

They argue back and forth, but my daddy gets his way. I can hear them trying to move that horse as Jamaica Bob walks past me toward a old beat-up truck.

I stare at the ground as he passes, and something catches my eye. It's a bracelet, thin and gold with a little butterfly on it. I remember when Mama bought it when we went to the fair one time. It musta come off when I was grabbin' at her arm.

I pick it up and pocket it. It's like a little piece of her she left behind.

Jamaica Bob's getting a rope outta the back of the pickup truck and tying it to the legs of the dead horse. It takes six guys to help out. Some neighbors watch from their stoops or windows, none too happy, especially when they start hosing off all that blood on the street.

My daddy stands silent, his back to me. He's wearing a white T, old jeans, and Timberland boots. His hair is short and nappy, his arms lean and strong. The gun still hangs by his side. The others get the horse tied to the bumper of the truck and start dragging it down the street.

Bob says, "Just put it behind the corral till we figure this out."

Everyone follows the horse and truck, leaving only me, Bob, and the man who's supposed to be my daddy.

Bob finally looks at me, then him, then back at me again. "Man! He even looks like you, Harp."

Daddy turns to me for the first time, sighs. He looks me up and down, makes a face. "Can't be mine. Too scrawny."

"Harp, I remember when you was twelve, and let me tell you, you was no Mike Tyson."

Harp grimaces at me, nods. "Coltrane."

I shake my head. "Nobody calls me that. It's Cole."

He smiles. "Yeah. Well, it seems like I been nobody to your mama your whole life, so I'm gonna call you by your proper name, since I gave it to you."

That's a new one.

"*You* named me? Why would you call me something stupid like Coltrane? Who ever heard of a name like *that*?"

Bob fans his face with his hat. "Man, the boy clearly don't know his jazz history."

Harp scowls. "Well, you can call me Harper. Then we'll be even."

He stares at the brick street, kicks at a old brick sticking out. "Look, I know you don't want to be here. And I can't say that I want you here neither. Heard you was in trouble . . . or maybe you *was* the trouble. Which is it?"

I shrug. He don't know me.

He shakes his head. "Before last night, I haven't heard from your moms in forever. Then she just calls me up out of the blue. . . ." He kicks the brick outta its hole in the ground.

I don't know what to say.

He mutters some swear word, picking up that brick and throwing it into a vacant lot. Then without looking at me, he says, "You can spend the night, and after that . . . we'll see what's what." He gazes up at the sky like he can't believe all of this was dumped in his lap on the same day. "In the meantime, you do what I say, and maybe I'll make it through the next couple days. Now get your bags and go on inside, *Coltrane.*"

He already gettin' on my nerves. But he the one holding a gun, so I just shut my trap and pick up my bags off the stoop.

FIVE

The front door's open. I walk in and the first thing I smell is . . . *horses*? I ain't never smelled a horse before, never even saw one up close before a few minutes ago. But if a horse got a smell, I think this is it, 'cause that's all that's in here: horse stuff. A coupla old saddles, blankets, brushes, work boots, horse things like you see on TV. Instead of furniture, there's even them square things of hay to sit on.

This ain't no house—it's a *barn*.

To top it off, there a big ol' hole from floor to ceiling knocked into the side of the living room, leading into the place next door, like he just wanted to expand his crib and took over the abandoned one next to his.

I peek inside the hole, but it's dark 'cause all the windows is boarded up. But man, it *really* smells like animal in there. Suddenly, something big moves in the dark, and I jump back.

"That's Lightning," says Harper.

My eyes adjust to a pair of dark eyes staring back at me.

It's a *horse*. He got a horse *in* the house.

No wonder Mama left him.

"Just temporary accommodations until I fix his stall. One of the stable walls kinda fell in last month. Lucky for me, next door's been boarded up for a while. Won't nobody mind if I'm using it."

Now I seen everything, I think. Harper must see my eyes buggin' out, 'cause he smirks and says, "Welcome to Philly, boy."

That feels like a dare, like he thinks I'm scared of that thing. That horse is *big*, bigger than any living thing I ever seen, but I ain't gonna let no horse show me up.

I drop my bags and take a step closer. The air is

thick and musty. My eyes get used to the dark, and I can see there's hay on the floor and a bucket of water near the wall. Lightning's staring at me with one big eye, his nostrils sniffing at me. His hoofs clomp on the floorboards.

I take another step, but the horse suddenly neighs and stomps his foot in front of me. I stumble back into the room and right into Harper.

Harper shakes his head like I just proved him right. "He don't like strangers. He's just used to living with me. You'll have to earn his trust."

I scowl. "Earn his trust? He just a horse!"

"And you just a boy," he says.

He gives me a long look. "Take your stuff upstairs. There's a space I cleared for you. Get settled, then come find me."

Then he walks out the door again, leaving me all alone with that monster.

"I ain't no boy," I say, but I go upstairs anyway, only 'cause I think horses can't climb steps. But up there ain't no better. These houses is tall and skinny—only one room wide. But that's just it, there's one room—*his* room, which got a bed, a bathroom, and a closet. I look in the closet and see he pulled stuff outta it and put a blanket on the floor.

Uh . . . *no*.

24

I ain't no Harry Potter. And I ain't living in no closet.

I got to think.

I look around for a phone, but there ain't one that I can see. Don't matter, I guess, since I can't call Mama anyways on account of she ain't home yet. And my friends ain't got no car, so they can't help me neither. Maybe they don't even know that I'm gone, since most of 'em drift in and out depending on if they in juvie or not. One more gone ain't gonna make a difference.

So I sit on the edge of the bed and bury my head in my hands. *What am I gonna do?* My head hurts, and my stomach aches. I just roll up on the bed and hope this is just some nasty dream that's gonna go away.

But after a hour, nothing changes.

My eyes wander around the room, stopping at a picture on his dresser. It's a young guy with a racehorse. It looks like Harper a long time ago. He at a racetrack next to a sign that says Philadelphia Park, standing in front of a horse with one of them fancy riders on top.

There's another picture, him riding a horse through the streets next to some pimped-out Caddie. Man, who ever heard of horses in the 'hood?

Then I notice a small picture in the back. I stand up to take a closer look. It's one of Mama, looking young and holding a baby. Is that me? I never seen this one. She standing in front of this house, I think. Only it looks a bit better than it do now.

A drop of water falls on the picture. I know it ain't no leak. I miss Mama, even though we ain't seen eye to eye lately . . . well, for a long time. But she was the only one who seemed to care about me when I was growing up. I never thought in a million years she'd turn on me. It's not like I killed someone or ended up in prison or something. When I think that she just left me here with dumb ol' black Clint Eastwood, I get mad all over again.

SIX

I take off my Pistons shirt and put on a white T. I'm hungry and he didn't even give me no food, so I guess I gotta fend for myself. But I'm looking through his fridge and there ain't nothing in there—just beer, cheese, and a pizza that looks like it's from last year.

I hope there's a McDonald's around here, 'cause I gots to eat! I'm about to head out when I remember, I ain't got no money. Dag. Now what?

That's when I see a envelope on the table with *Harper* written on it.

It's Mama's handwriting.

I open it. There's a note inside and . . . money. Maybe two hundred dollars.

The note says: *This is all I got on me for now. Use it to feed Cole. I took care of him for twelve years. It's now up to you to help him find his way.*

I stare at that money for a good twenty minutes. That money could get me back home again. Back to where I belong. But the way she talk about me at the end of that note . . . it just makes me wanna crawl into a hole and die. Why should I go back if she don't want me? Plus she would just yell at me for stealing this money . . . 'cept it's not stealing, 'cause she said it was for taking care of me.

When I get depressed, I eat. So I pocket twenty bucks. I gotta get some food in me. Then I can figure out what I'm gonna do.

I step outside and look around. I see a buncha girls on the sidewalk jumping rope. They stop and stare at me, so I just stare right back. But just past them is the two guys who was making fun of me before, sittin' on a stoop and jawin' away. So I turn around and walk down the block the other way.

This neighborhood is just like ours in Detroit, only the buildings is older row houses made a brick. Some is closed up and vacant, covered in graffiti. Others got bars on the windows. I put on my mad-dog face so nobody will mess with me. I just gotta follow the rules of the street: Rule one: Keep your head down. Rule two: Always keep moving.

"Hey!" someone calls out from behind me.

I ignore 'em like I didn't hear.

"Hey!" I hear footsteps coming up fast.

I think of running, but that's rule three: Never run. I whip around and see the two guys looking at me. The tall one with cornrows is grinning.

"What?!" I yell.

He gives me a look that says, *Don't be giving me attitude or I'll give you a beatin'.* But I hold my ground.

"You know who I am?" he says.

I shake my head and look for a way out. His buddy, who's big and stocky like a linebacker, just stares at me.

The tall guy takes a pretend swing at me, and I flinch. He laughs. "Tough guy from Motown. I'm your cousin Smush."

"Smush? I don't know no cousin Smush."

He rolls his eyes. "On your daddy's side. You're Uncle Harp's boy, right? That mean we related, cuz, which is good for you. Otherwise I'd have to have Snapper here put out a Chester Avenue welcome for ya. And you don't want that."

Snapper looks disappointed. He knocks me in the shoulder, but friendly-like. "Didn't mean to give you a hard time in front of your moms."

Smush giggles. "Oh, yes you did! Don't lie."

Snapper smiles a little and shrugs. "Your moms really just dumped you off and left you? That's cold."

Smush puts his arm around me. He tall, so my head's just under his arm. "Listen, if you staying here, you gotta know the lay of the land. Where you off to? The stables?"

I give him a look. "Stables? I ain't no ghetto cowboy."

That cracks them up. "Oh, dang!" says Smush. "Did you hear that? Better not let your daddy hear you talking that way."

"I don't care. He ain't my daddy. I never seen him before, and he don't want me here, which is fine by me."

I turn and start walking.

"Yo, cuz, wait up. You don't wanna be going that way. You might get yourself shot."

I stop. "I ain't afraid."

"Cuz, you don't get it. Here on Chester Avenue, we in the safe zone, on account of the horses. The gangbangers leave this block alone, outta respect, ya know? Plus your daddy don't put up with none of them! Believe me, I know." He rubs his butt like it's been kicked one too many times.

Snapper shakes his head. "Shorty, you go out there, a few blocks either way, it's a war zone. You got to watch your back, know what I'm sayin'?"

Smush nods. "Yeah, you fresh meat around here, cuz, so you better go see your daddy. He at the stable over there."

I look down the street and see a bunch of run-down garages across from a vacant lot with some homemade buildings and fences and stuff. There's a few kids washing horses on the sidewalk.

"What kinda place is this?"

Smush and Snapper laugh. "You'll get used to it. Horses always been here."

"Whatever." I don't feel like going into a war zone, so I start walking to the stable.

I walk slowly past the kids washing the horses. They younger than me, maybe seven or eight. They all frontin' and boastin' about racing and stuff.

"I'ma be next to fly down the Speedway!" says the smallest one.

The oldest one laughs. "You gotta learn to ride first! You can't even stay on Daisy!"

The middle one drops his hose in a bucket. "Harp say he gonna get me a Thoroughbred over at New Holland. Then I'm gonna leave you fools in the dirt!" They all laugh.

I try and joke with 'em. "Where I come from, kids wash cars." They stop laughing and look at me.

The oldest one says, "You wanna help? Harp'll let you ride if you help out with the horses."

I wave 'em off. "Nah. I ain't stayin'. And I ain't ridin' no dang horse. What you thinkin' ridin' a horse in the city? I already seen one get hit by a car, and I just got here. "

They look at each other like I don't know what I'm talking about and just start yappin' about racing horses again. I look up and see a whole row of sneakers hanging from the telephone wire overhead. That's exactly how I feel: hung out to dry.

SEVEN

The stables is nothing more than a few garages and some vacant lots with old buildings that look like they made outta scrap. I peek inside one. It's dark and smells all dank like horse. There's banged-up plywood and hay on the floor, and the ceiling is covered in cobwebs so thick, it looks like nobody ever cleaned up there before. The stalls is small, with no windows, and the wood is old and warped, like it's been there forever. There's maybe ten horses inside, all poking their heads outta their cubbyholes, looking at me like *I'm* the one who shouldn't be in the city. Why they need horses out here, anyhow? I don't get it.

I hear some whistling outside and go around back to check it out. I spot a black horse running around all crazy inside a circular fence. A few guys and a bunch of kids hang off the fence whooping it up and making noise. They ain't dressed like cowboys, just regular street clothes. One of the guys even dresses like them Muslim dudes, in a black robe and skullcap.

The horse is kicking and stomping at something. He looks wild, all black and rough, ready to do some damage. When I walk up to the fence, I see it's Harper inside there, all alone with that crazy thing!

His white T is covered with dirt, his hair too. He just standing there in the ring watching that horse almost run him over every time it circles him. Man, I knew he was crazy. He gonna get himself killed for real. Then what'll happen to me?

But Harper acts all calm, like it ain't no big thing, following the horse with his eyes as he steps right into the horse's path. The horse skids to a stop and suddenly, they face-to-face. I think for sure the horse is going to charge him, but Harper just raises his hands, nice and easy. Everyone watching gets all quiet.

When he steps closer, the horse backs up, almost into the fence. Harp reaches forward to touch him, and the horse suddenly jumps up on his back legs, like he gonna stomp him. But Harper don't back off. He stands there, as calm as can be, like he reeling the monster in with his mind. He starts whispering something over and over until that horse finally settles back down to earth. The kids shake their heads like they can't believe what they seein'.

Harper moves in closer and closer, the horse rising up a coupla times. But suddenly Harper's standing right next to him, his hand on the horse's shoulder, then his neck, and finally, his head. Harper shushes him like a little baby till the horse is all relaxed, and then it's just the two of them together. Harper's all smiles, patting the horse on his neck. Then he sees me. He walks the horse over my way, where it comes right up shaking its head at me. I jump off the fence.

"You ever seen a real-live horse before you got here?"

I step back a few feet. "Nah. I live in the city."

He laughs. "This *is* the city."

I roll my eyes. "This ain't no city. This is like . . . I don't know what. It's crazy, all I know."

The Muslim dude grins. "That your son?"

Harper shakes his head. "Nah, just found him on my doorstep." He turns back to me. "Wanna ride?"

"You crazy? I ain't getting on one a them things!"

He points to the kids sitting on the fence. "See them kids? They smaller than you, but they all ride."

I look at them. They look just like any kids you might find flippin' on a mattress in any ol' empty lot. They don't look afraid, pattin' that horse from the fence. But I still ain't getting up on something that's ten times bigger than me. "Nah. I'm too hungry now. I ain't eaten since yesterday."

Then someone behind me says, "Is that so?"

I turn around and see a old head, looking at me all close-up through thick beat-up glasses, his big ol' cowboy hat almost hittin' me in the head. He must be a hundred years old.

He squints at me. "Harper, you didn't feed this boy?"

Harper shrugs. "Can't you see I'm busy? Boy can fend for himself."

The old man shakes his head, whispers to me. "Dang fool. Don't care about nobody unless they got four legs and a tail. Come on, I got some eats in the clubhouse. Follow me."

I follow the old man. He got real dark skin, which make his white hair look like snow. His legs seem all crooked, like he been knocked off a horse one too many times. On the way over, he starts giving me a tour of the place. "We got us three stables on this property, 'bout thirty stalls total. We're full up at the moment, since some of the other stables 'round here closed in the last couple years."

He stops and waves at another old-timer who's playing chess by himself. "Must be forty or so of us riders who call this home, though some guys is too old to ride much," he says. "This fella here got knocked off his horse about three months ago, ain't that right, Doc? We found him lying on his back, his shoes still stuck in the stirrups of his horse!" They laugh and shake hands. "Thought he was dead, but he was up and about and just fine after a few days. Tough dude, this one."

We pass a few other kids stacking them hay squares. They look kinda scraggly, like they was playin' in the dirt, but happy. Like them other kids, they talking about who's the fastest racer. The old man jokes with them, "Y'all owe me sodas from falling off your horse, so you shouldn't be talking about who's the fastest just yet. 'Sides, we all know who the fastest *really* is." He points at himself, and they all laugh and give him high fives.

"Them your kids?" I ask as we move on.

He smiles. "My kids? Well, I practically raised 'em since they was pups, but nah, they ain't mine. My kids is too busy working for their corporate masters to be concerned with horses." He sees I got no idea what he talking about. "These kids here come off the streets. They got nowhere else to go, 'cept gangs."

A stray cat comes wandering up to him, and he picks it up. I notice there's a lot of strays running around here. "Kids and cats. They seem to find their way here, and they keep coming back. What're you gonna do?"

He hobbles around a corner, where I see a homemade shack. "Well, here we are." The "clubhouse" is a old one-room shed with a dirt floor. We go inside, where the old man has a coupla plug-in cookers going . . . but it actually smells pretty good.

"Got some Texas chili with cowboy potatoes over rice and homemade corn bread. You like corn bread?"

"Right now, as long as it ain't movin', I'll eat it."

He blows the dust out of a old bowl and fills it up. "Boys got to eat!" he says, laughing.

We sit down on some old folding chairs, and he watches me dig in. Food's good too, not like what I normally eat. It makes my stomach feel all warm.

He sees me looking at some old pictures of a black cowboy on the wall.

"That's me, back in the day. Used to be the number-one bull rider on the southwest tour."

I think he musta watched one too many cowboy movies on TV. "Sure thing, mister. . . ."

"What, you don't believe me?"

I swallow my food. "Look, you guys might think y'all is cowboys, but all I know is, real cowboys is white."

The old man shakes his head, like I'm a fool. "Son, don't you know black cowboys is a tradition that goes back to before the Civil War?"

"Whatever," I say.

He looks disappointed. "Not whatever, man. The word *cowboy* started as a *black* word. Wear it proudly."

"So how come I never seen any black cowboys on TV then?"

He waves his hand. "TV. Humph. Can't trust the media to tell the truth. The truth is, the white man always gets his way. Looky here. . . ."

He pulls out a book from a dusty shelf. It got pictures and drawings from a long time ago. He shows me some old black-and-white pictures of black dudes dressed in homemade clothes doing cowboy stuff— roping, riding, and cleaning horses.

"Back in the slave days, the slave who worked in the house was called a *houseboy*. The slaves who worked with the cows was called *cowboys*. Get it?"

No, but he just getting started. He points to a picture of a black cowboy riding a horse out in the wild. He got one of them cowboy rope things whirling in the air like he about to catch some bull. "That's Bill Pickett, son of a slave and the most famous black cowboy of all. Back then, there was almost nine thousand black cowboys out West, working cattle and driving 'em up the Chisholm Trail and such. And these cowboys was so good that eventually, the whites took the name *cowboy* for themselves. Stole it, really. Now we're just trying to take it back, is all."

He straightens his hat, like he in a movie or something.

I shake my head. "You guys is funny. We in the city, with cars and computers and stuff, and you think you back in the *Wild, Wild West!*"

He smiles, like *I'm* the one living in a fantasy world.

I shrug and start eating again. He watches me for a long time until I say, "Why you gotta stare at me for?"

That makes him laugh. "You got your mama's eyes, but your daddy's attitude."

I choke on something, and he lean over and smacks me on the back. "You know my mama?" I ask.

"Know her? I'm the one who drove her back to her folks in Detroit."

This is definitely news to me. "Why'd you do *that*?" I say, my face gettin' all hot.

He looks at me like I hurt his feelings or something. "I didn't drive her away—I just took her home to her people, like she asked me to. See, sometimes young'uns aren't up for the things they get themselves into. I know your daddy well, known him his whole life. He can take care of a horse better'n anybody, but a wife and a kid? He was useless. It was the best thing for you."

Just thinking about Harp caring more for a dumb

horse than us gets me seein' red. "What'd I ever do to him?"

He bends down close to me and whispers, "You didn't do nothing, son. You was only a tiny guy. Some people just relate better to animals. But your mama, she don't got horse in her blood. She tried, but I knew it was gonna end badly. It don't make either side bad; it's just the way it is. Sometimes you gotta move on."

That makes me even more mad 'cause I realize me and Harper got something in common: we both drove Mama away.

EIGHT

The old man pats me on the back. "Harp said he and your mama are gonna talk again tonight on the phone. We'll get this mess cleaned up, don't you worry. Meanwhile, eat up, then come on out and ask for me. Name's Tex."

I watch him shuffle out, and I just sit there, shakin' my head. *Great. Texas in Philly now.* I finish up my bowl, and just when I start thinkin' about what I'm gonna do next, Harper walks in.

He has a brush in one hand and a rake in the other. He hands the brush to me. "If you gonna be here today, might as well make yourself useful."

I look at the brush. "I don't think so."

He acts like I didn't say nothing. "It's a horse brush. Go out front and help brush down the horses. The kids'll show you how."

I shake my head. "Nah-uh. I ain't going near them horses. I seen how you almost got stomped on this morning."

He smirks. "That's whatcha call re-starting a horse. Some of 'em that we bring in are pretty nervous and out of control 'cause of what they been through at the tracks."

I can see he not going to go away. "What's wrong with 'em?" I ask.

"Nothing, they just been abandon—" He catches himself, starts again. "They're old racehorses that normally get sold off for meat. We pool our money to buy what we can at auction before the slaughterhouse gets 'em. Then we bring 'em here so they can live out their days—the kids learn to ride, and we get a few more horses to race with. 'Course, with money being tight an' all . . ."

But my mind's still stuck on the meat part. "People *eat* horses?" I ask.

"Dogs. They get sold for dog food."

I feel like I been sold for dog food, but I still ain't getting near them things. "I'll just stay here, thanks," I say.

He shakes his head. "The heck you will. If you here, you gotta help out. Everybody works. All those kids work and so will you."

I don't say nothing, just stare hard at that brush.

He can see I really got my mind set, 'cause after a few seconds, he holds out the rake. "Fine . . . then go muck the stalls in the Ritz-Carlton instead."

I'm confused until I find out the Ritz-Carlton is what they call the main stable. They call it that as a joke 'cause it's definitely *not* a luxury hotel. In fact, when I see it, I know this as far from luxury as a horse can get. It looks more like a dungeon, all dark and cramped. And a homemade dungeon at that, since it's held together by old doors and scrap wood from torn-down buildings. *And* it smells funky.

When I see what needs cleaning up, I think, *No way.* There's piles of muck all over — and I mean the kind that come out of a horse. Man, these things must eat a lot. Harper leaves me there, with the rake and a wheelbarrow and says I got till sundown to finish picking up all this crap.

I stand there for five minutes, then decide I'll do what he says for *today* . . . but tomorrow, I'm outta here. I don't know how, but one way or another, I'll get back to Motor City. But the second I step into one of them stalls, I know I made the wrong choice to work in the barn. My white Nikes is all covered in greenish-brown you-know-what in about a minute. I'll never get 'em cleaned.

I start working. Even though this sucks for sure, I just keep going, nonstop, 'cause if I stop, I'll start thinking about how my mama just up and left me with a stranger. And a strange stranger too, even if he supposed to be my dad.

So I work and feel the burn in my arms, the sweat on my back. I don't care. I'll make her feel sorry for leaving me behind to clean up this stuff.

The only good thing right now is all them horses is outside. But just doing the one stall takes me 'bout a hour. When I fill up the cart, I wheel it out to find out where to dump it. I run into Jamaica Bob.

"Where do all this go?" I ask him. He waves me to follow him, but don't offer to help me push. We turn the corner, and my jaw drops open.

Behind the barn is a mountain. Not a mountain like with snow on it and stuff. This is a mountain of *horse crap*. I ain't kidding you. This thing is about fifteen feet tall and fills up a huge part of the yard.

Bob scowls. "City used to come and haul it away, just like it did for all the stables in Philly. Then about two months ago, they just up and stopped, saying something about budget issues and how we ain't legal—"

"Legal? What you mean?" I ask.

He makes a face. "We own some of these structures here, but all of *this* land," he says, pointing from the Ritz to the corral and the clubhouse, all the way out to the fields, where some teenagers are running horses. "The City owns all *that*. But it never did anything with it, 'cause nobody ever wanted nothing to do with this neighborhood. For decades, they just let it rot. Buildings would sit here empty and vandalized, just waiting to become crack houses and gang hangouts. But this our home turf, and we decided to make something of it. So we took it back. Made it our own."

My eyes bug out. "You *stole* it from the City?"

He leans in real close to make sure I hear him right. "No. We reclaimed it. It's called homesteading—that means if they don't use it, they lose it."

I look around the spread. "I didn't know you could do that."

"We turned something ugly into something beautiful, Cole. Turned it into a real neighborhood. It's the only safe place around here, the only place a kid can go without worrying about messing with guns. And it's all 'cause of them horses."

My eyes come to rest on that smelly mountain in front of me. "But what you gonna do now? How much bigger is that pile gonna get?"

He laughs bitterly. "A lot, because the City suddenly decided it wanted to build a mall and condos out here. Now it wants the land back."

I'm confused. "What's that got to do with *this*?" I say, pointing at the pile.

He takes his hat off, wipes his brow. "Everything." He looks up and sees a neighbor staring out her window at him. She don't look happy and shuts her curtains.

"See, the neighbors always liked us, but now they see this . . . *pile* . . . growing in the heat and humidity of summer, where it smells ten times worse and . . . well, you get the picture. City stopped service in order to divide us. Then all they gotta do is wait for the complaints to start rolling in, and next thing ya know, *BOOM,* they swoop in with health code violations—"

He stops, must see he lost me. Shrugs.

"Just shovel this onto the pile. It won't matter much, 'cause they'll be coming to shut us down soon."

Before I can say *Why?* he gestures over to something covered with a tarp.

My jaw drops again when I see a hoof sticking out from underneath the tarp. "Is that—?"

"Yep. But we got nowhere to take it, just like we got nowhere to haul this pile. And it ain't even our horse." He spits. "Yep, the end is coming, that much I know. . . ."

NINE

I start rolling that wheelbarrow back and forth. Fill it, empty it, fill it, empty it. I don't care.

Slowly them other kids bring back the horses they was washing to put them in the stalls. The oldest one smiles when he sees me working. "I guess Harp told you everybody works if they come in here."

"I just felt sorry for y'all. I still ain't stayin'," I say as I roll up to the last stall. I hear a noise and peek into the stall where that horse Harper broke is standing—big, black, sweaty, and staring me down.

I freeze in my tracks just as Harper comes strolling in with a bunch of hay. "You 'bout done?"

He takes the hay into the stall, but the horse is still staring right at me and starts backing into the corner.

"I think he's scared of you," says Harp.

Yeah, I don't think so. He just wants me to come closer so he can stomp on me.

Harper sees me frozen there. "Boy, if you gonna be around horses, you gotta learn they ain't gonna hurt you unless you scared. A horse can smell fear; it makes 'em nervous. You scared?"

I look at him. "Who you calling scared?"

He shakes his head. "Nobody, unless you *are* scared. Now, come here."

I take a few steps in, and the horse snorts and backs up to the wall.

Harper hands me some hay. "Hold it out for him."

I look at Harper like he crazy.

"He's not gonna bite you. Just do it."

I hold it up, and the horse looks at it.

"Say something to him. He'll come."

My mind goes blank. "Like what?"

He rolls his eyes. "What would you say to a dog?" he asks.

That is one big dog. "Uh . . . come here, boy?"

"You got it." He nods.

And with that, Harper walks out.

"Hey." I turn around, but he gone. Then I feel a tug on my arm. I turn slowly and see the biggest head I ever seen on anything right in front of my face.

I can't move.

The horse's big ol' nose is sniffing me. I can feel it huffin' and puffin', its nostrils opening up like they gonna suck me right in. Then it raises its head and *CHOMP*, these giant teeth start pulling at the hay in my hand, chewin' away, his big ol' eyes staring at me. It bites closer to my hand, and I let go. He follows the hay to the ground and he keeps eating, like I ain't even there.

This thing is huge. I just stare at his giant yellow teeth as they crunch away. He do kinda act like a dog, so I slowly put my hand on his neck like Harper done. He don't flinch. His hair is rough like doll hair, but the fur on his neck is soft and smooth.

"Good boy . . ." I whisper.

I think about how Harper talked to the horse earlier. I let my hand move up to his neck and keep saying, "Good boy, good boy." He moves his hoof and almost steps on my foot. I can feel his weight when that hoof goes down. That makes me nervous, like maybe he don't know how big he is. But when I look back up at his face, he looking right at me, and then I know he knows that I'm there. And suddenly I don't feel so scared no more.

TEN

I finish up and wait for Harper. Outside the barn door, I can see the sun turning orange as it gets low in the sky. Sun feels different here than in Detroit, bigger maybe. I can see the downtown buildings way off in the distance, the freeway hustling nearby.

I hear a bang go off in the distance. I think it's a car backfiring, but then a few more go off and I know it's gunshots. That much is the same as Detroit. Pretty soon, I hear a 'copter chopping overhead. I can feel it in my body as it whooshes by. It ain't going far.

Harper pops his head in. "Time to go." I'm covered in dirt and who knows what. He nods, like he approves. "You'll feel it in the morning."

Harp closes up the barn and puts some other stuff in the storage room while I spend about ten minutes cleaning the muck from my Nikes.

When we walk out onto the street, I notice all the kids is gone. About ten of the guys is left, gathered around a fire in a trash can on the vacant lot across the way, sittin' on a old couch and chair somebody left behind. Some of them is Harper's age, but they dress different—wearing goatees and shades, black cowboy hats, Levi jackets, and boots. They look tall and serious, like a cowboy Malcolm X. They knocking back some brews, talking trash about some race coming up at a place called the Speedway.

The Muslim guy, who ain't drinking, waves to Harper. "Hey, you letting Lightning out tomorrow?"

Harper smiles, all sly. "Who wants to know?"

The Muslim dude laughs, points to another guy I ain't seen before, a dude as big as Notorious B.I.G., wearing a red Phillies jacket.

"Big Dee says he's got a hundred riding on a Lightning-Rocket rematch."

Tex pipes in, egging Harper on. "That is if you ain't too *scared*. . . ."

The other guys start chanting, *Race, race, race.*

I can tell Harper likes the attention.

Big Dee holds up his big hand. "When you gonna

grace us with your presence, Harp? It's been three months, man!"

Harper smiles. "You know, once you been king for so long, it gets kinda old. Besides, Lightning's just been resting up till y'all recover from your last humiliation."

The guys all bust up. They know a good smackdown when they hear it.

The Muslim guy pipes in. "I don't know, man. Rocket's been looking *goood* lately. Big Dee got a new rider an' all."

Harper raises a eyebrow. "Yeah? And who that be?"

Big Dee grins, his eyes hidden behind his shades. "Come on down and find out for yourself, man."

Harper acts all amused. He glances at me, winks. "Maybe I will, just to show the boy here what speed really looks like."

That gets a big reaction. The guys really whoop it up. Harper starts walking away, and Big Dee adds, "Maybe your boy can handle that horse better than you."

Harper laughs at that one. A little too much. I give him a look, but he keeps walking and laughing like that's the funniest thing he ever heard.

. . .

I follow Harper to his house. The sky is turning purple and darkness is coming on fast. People who was out earlier is now clearing from the streets. If it's anything like where I'm from, I know you don't wanna be out after dark or some fool might clip you by accident.

When we get back in his house, Harper locks it up good and tight. As soon as the sun sets, I can hear the streets coming to life again. The booming bass of a car passing by rattles the walls. I feel all jumpy and Lightning acts nervous too, but Harper calms him down.

Now that I got nothing to do, my mind starts thinking again, remembering what's up. "When you gonna call Mama?" I ask.

He stops petting Lightning. "I get to it later."

That won't do. I know she home by now. "You better call her. I can take a bus back or something."

He stands there a moment, not saying nothing.

So I keep talking. "I know she over it by now. Probly feels all lonely in our apartment, wondering what the heck she did and—"

"She ain't coming back, Coltrane."

I ignore him. "She be sitting all by herself, eating

some frozen dinner, thinking she'll come get me tomorrow. . . ."

"There ain't gonna be no tomorrow. She's not coming."

I look at him good. "How you know that if you ain't called her yet?"

For the first time, he don't look so tough. I can see him struggling to figure out what to say.

"What?" I ask.

"Your mama called me a couple hours ago."

A car comes booming up the road, setting the windows a-shaking. Harp come right up to me. "She called me, saying she had a long time to think about it and how even though she don't care for me any, she knows this is a better place for you. She's got other things to deal with right now."

This is like a bomb going off in my head. How long she gonna play this game? "Nah . . . she just saying that to mess with you. She be back."

"Coltrane, I know this woman. When she makes up her mind, it's done."

"I know her too. I know she loves me and would never give me up for good. She would never—"

"Coltrane!" he yells.

I jump back.

He grinds his teeth. "I waited for years for her to come back, but it never happened. She's a strong-headed woman, and she means what she says."

My mind is racing. I don't wanna hear him talk no more. "She didn't come back 'cause she don't love you. Whatever you done to her isn't like what's going on between me and her."

"Yeah? Well, what *is* going on between you and her? What kind of kid drives his mama to the point where she can't deal with you no more? You on drugs? In a gang? Do you hit her? What?" He towering over me now, but I don't care. He can't hurt me.

I push him away. "I ain't do nothing to her!"

Suddenly I'm out in the street, the door banging behind me. All I can think of is, *I'm outta here! I don't need him! I just need to get back home.*

I start running. I hear him call out, "Coltrane!" but I keep moving. I don't even look back.

ELEVEN

I turn the corner. The street is dark. I take a few steps and realize I got no idea where I am. I look each way, but it all looks the same.

When I was small, Mama told me if I ever got lost to just close my eyes and listen and I would hear her calling. But I ain't looking for her now. I'm looking for a main street. I close my eyes. What I hear is . . . music . . . yelling . . . a helicopter . . . but then I hear it—traffic.

I open my eyes, and it seem brighter down the way I'm looking, like maybe there's a big street down there. So I take off running.

A car passes me then slows up ahead, its red taillights feeling like some kinda warning. I think about what Smush said earlier about this neighborhood, and I turn at the corner, 'cause right now I don't wanna talk to no 'bangers.

I see people on their stoops, staring at me, but I keep my head down and keep moving. A few blocks later, I see a big street ahead. When I hit the corner, I smell something that reminds me of home—the Golden Arches.

I'm thinking I ain't eaten nothing since that old guy fed me. I feel in my pocket and my hand touches that twenty-dollar bill. I need fuel so I can get my head straight.

I stuff my face on the dollar menu—three double cheeseburgers, a apple pie, a Coke. I pound that stuff down, and I start to realize I only got fourteen dollars left.

How'm I gonna get back to Detroit on that?

Take a bus? That's gotta cost at least a hundred.

Hitchhike? Who gonna pick up a punk like me?

Walk? That'd take me a month.

Unless I can get my hands on the rest of that money Harper got, I'll be stuck here for good. *Why didn't I just grab it when the grabbin' was good?*

I sit in that McDonald's for a coupla hours. Every time the manager starts looking at me, I get something else to eat. I know I can't stay here all night, but where I'm gonna go? I don't wanna go back to Harper's. I know he don't want me, just like Mama don't want me, and this manager chump ain't no different.

Maybe I could find my cousin Smush, but I got no idea where he lives. No, I got to find a place to lay low. Then in the morning, when Harper leaves the house, I can snag the rest of the money Mama left behind.

I hop a fence and I'm in the back area by the stables, the only place I can think of where nobody will be at tonight. But then I see a light on in the clubhouse.

I sneak up to the window, which is so clouded with dirt, I don't think it's ever been washed. I peek inside and see Tex, all by himself on a cot watching a little TV set. I wonder if he lives here or if he just like a night guard or something. I think maybe Harper'll end up like this too, all alone with them horses.

I sneak over to the Ritz-Carlton and open the door a crack. It's a full moon, so it lights up enough for me to see. I hear the horses shuffle a little. Then I see the horse I petted today. He perks up, looking at me like he was all lonely before I walked in. He leans forward, expecting me to feed him too. I pull out the apple pie I got in my pocket. I was gonna save it for later, but what the heck. He takes it, chomps it down in one bite. So much for dessert.

This seem as good a place as any to hole up in till morning. There's a few things of hay around, so I arrange it like a bed across from the stalls and throw a horse blanket over it. If nobody wants me, I'll sleep with the horses. Least they appreciate me.

But sleeping in a barn ain't like sleeping in your bed. There's lots of noise going on all around you, and the horses sometime get skittish. They all looking at me, like, *Why's he here?*

Why not? I think. Can't be any worse than sleeping in a closet.

But it still takes me a long time to fall asleep.

TWELVE

Something brushes by me, and my eye opens. The sun is up, but I can barely move, my body's so stiff. I look down, and somebody left me a pack of Pop-Tarts and a orange juice.

"Breakfast of champions."

I look up and see Tex standing there. "What time is it?"

"'Bout seven thirty," he answers. "I hope you aren't gonna make a habit of sleeping here. Your daddy called looking for you, and I told him I saw you come in last night. Told him maybe you thought this really *was* the Ritz-Carlton."

Funny. For a old blind guy, he got eyes in the back of his head. "Sorry," I say, but I don't really feel like explaining nothing.

"Well, eat up. Harp's gonna be here in a few, then you'll get your first peek at the Speedway. Saturday's race day."

I tell him I ain't interested in racing. Never seen a race and don't care to. He just laughs.

Tex wanders over to my horse friend and opens up his stall. I grab the OJ and Pop-Tarts, thinking he gonna start bucking.

The old man chuckles. "He's okay. I think he's taking a liking to you. Go over there and call him."

I think the old man is joking, but he ain't. I walk over by the door, but I don't know what to say. The dog thing seem stupid now.

"Just call his name," Tex says.

"What's his name?" I ask.

Tex scratches his chin. "Hmm, I guess we haven't come up with one yet. Tell you what—why don't you name him?"

I look around. "Who, me?"

"Why not? You both strays. Who better?"

The horse stands there looking at me, his hair sticking up all over the place, like he just woke up too, but his eyes is wide open. For some reason, I think of Boo, 'cause he looks like someone just scared him.

"What about Boo?" I say, and the old man gives him the once-over.

"Looks like someone just gave him a good fright, don't it?" He smiles. "Let's give it a try. Call him over."

I take a few steps back. "Here, Boo. Come here, boy. . . ."

The horse tilts his head.

The old man reaches into his jacket and pulls out a carrot. "Try this."

He tosses it to me, and I hold it out.

"Here, Boo."

Boo takes a step and then another. Next thing I know, he right in front of me, munching on that thing. Just like a dog.

"Well, ain't that a picture."

I turn around, and Harper's sitting on top of Lightning, shaking his head. "Maybe you got horse blood in you after all."

THIRTEEN

I don't know if Harper's joking or if he serious, but I ain't in no mood to ask. I drop the carrot, walk back to my hay bed, and sit down. "Horse blood? Don't you remember? I'm the drug-dealin' gangbanger who hits his mom."

He watches me closely but don't dish nothing back. "Maybe you want to come with me to the Speedway. Might be better than sitting around in an old barn."

I wouldn't mind getting out of this stinky place. But I don't gotta be happy about it. "Whatever."

He reaches into a saddlebag and pulls something out. "Then you better wear these."

A pair of cowboy boots plop on the ground next to my feet. I give him a look.

"You think I'm gonna wear those?"

The old man picks them up and whistles. "Ain't these the boots I gave you when you was a little punk who showed up here acting all street?" He turns to me. "He didn't wear them either. But it's better getting these boots dirty than your white sneakers. See?" He holds up the boots and slides his fingers along the smooth bottom. "Crap just slides off, not like what's sticking in the nooks and crannies of your shoes."

I look at the bottom of my Nikes and see they ain't never gonna get clean again. He holds out the boots, but I ain't wearing them.

Tex shrugs. "Too bad. I wish I had a pair this nice."

Harper hops off of Lightning and ties him to a post. "Tex, help Coltrane get that horse saddled up. He's going riding today."

Tex shakes his head. "You do it. Least you can do is teach your own boy."

Harper scowls. "I don't think this boy wants to hear what I got to say."

But Tex is gone out the back way.

Harper smirks. "Look, you want to stay here at the

Ritz, fine. But you might as well learn a thing or two about horses while you're living with 'em, all right?"

I don't say nothing, just stand there. He claps his hands, like I just agreed with him. "All right! First we gonna need that blanket you slept on last night."

I get up. "You can have the blanket. But I ain't gettin' up on Boo."

"Boo?" he says. "Who named him Boo?"

I look around for Tex. "I guess I did."

He thinks about it, nods. "You named him; you ride him."

"Uh, I don't know if you noticed, but I ain't no cowboy."

But he just ignores me. Grabs a saddle off of a barrel. Then stands by the horse, waiting. "Come on, throw that blanket up here."

I think about just walking away. Then he starts laughing. At me.

"What, you aren't afraid, are you?"

I grab the blanket. "I'm from Detroit. I ain't afraid of nobody. People 'fraid of me."

The horse takes a dump right in front of us, and Harper laughs again.

"I guess that's why you called him Boo. You done scared that right out of him!"

I shake my head and throw the blanket up over Boo.

"Yeah, maybe I did, old man."

He tosses the saddle up on Boo's back, straightens everything out. "Look, I don't expect you to call me Daddy. But an old man I ain't. I'm thirty-seven."

He reaches under and grabs the strap from the other side of the saddle. He grunts.

Like I said—old man, I think.

He buckles it together and makes sure it's tight but not too tight. "That all right for you, Boo?" he asks.

Boo don't seem to mind.

"Hand me them stirrup straps."

I look around and see some things that look about right. He takes them and attaches 'em to the saddle.

"This is where you put your feet."

I shrug, like, *Why you telling me that? I still ain't going up there.*

He grabs some rope-and-steel thing off the wall and walks up to Boo's face. "Smile, Boo!"

He puts the steel up to Boo's mouth, and he opens. Boo chomps on it a bit, like he ain't had one in his mouth for a while.

Harper pats him on the neck. "He don't mind. He's used one his whole life, I bet."

Harp strings the rope back to the saddle, double-checks all the straps, and then nods. "That'll do, Boo." He turns and looks at me. "Ready, Freddy?"

He must think I look worried or something.

"It's no sweat, man," he says. "I take little kids for rides all the time. You ain't a little kid, are you?"

I push him out the way. "What you think?"

He shakes his head. "More like a punk if you ask me."

FOURTEEN

I grab the knob on top of the saddle and start to climb, but Boo starts moving around.

"Sit, Boo!" I yell.

Harper starts laughing his head off, then apologizes when I glare at him.

"Sorry, man. It's just . . ." He grabs the rope and steadies Boo, then points. "See that? Your foot goes in there, then you grab here, then you swing yourself up."

"I know what to do," I say, knowing I don't.

He sees me struggling to get my foot high enough into that thing. "Maybe you be better off on a pony," he says.

"I can do it," I say. I bring my foot *waaay* up and use my other hand to get it in there, then I reach way over to grab the saddle. It takes me two or three tries before I can climb up, but when I do . . . whoa.

My head is suddenly up near the cobwebs. I ain't never been this high before. And I definitely ain't never been on the back of a living thing like this.

"You okay up there?"

I nod.

"Just relax. Breathe," he says. "Don't hold on to the saddle so tight. Use this." He hands me the rope. Then he guides Boo slowly out into the open.

I gotta duck my head, but when we get outside, it's a whole different view from up here. It's like I'm ten feet tall all of a sudden. With each step, Boo's body swings back and forth and I think he just gonna fall over and that will be that. I think about the horse Mama hit and think if Boo falls on me, I'll be a goner.

Harper swings up on Lightning and moves over next to Boo. "We just going to take it slow, maybe go a few times around the corral, then head out."

It feels like I'm sitting on one of them giant walking machines in *Star Wars*.

"Just pretend you're part of the horse. Be like

Jell-O—swing your hips the way he walks, but keep the top half of you straight. Don't worry—I won't let you fall."

I don't say nothing. We go around the corral a couple a times, nice and easy, but just as I feel like this is all right, a plastic bag blows in front of us and Boo freaks out and bolts.

I grab on to the saddle, and he start running around in circles, almost squishing my leg against the fence. I'm bouncing up and down, barely holding on, the saddle hitting my butt. I'm thinking of jumping—but suddenly Harper's right there, riding alongside. He grabs the reins and slows Boo up till we come to a standstill.

My heart is beating a million miles a hour.

"You okay?" he asks.

I'm still alive, so I nod. "I'm done," I say, looking for a way down.

"Hold up there, Coltrane. You're okay. Just had a little excitement is all. For some reason, plastic bags unnerve the horses when they first get here. That's just one of those city things they never seen before. But when we head out, I'm going to tie a leash to Boo and that won't happen again. Promise."

Before I can change my mind, he ties a long rope to Boo's saddle and holds the other end, like he's gonna take us out for a walk. Tex comes out with a white cowboy hat. "Don't forget your lucky hat."

Harp smiles and puts it on. I give him a look, but he just tips his hat, all cool. "Gotta represent," he says.

When Lightning starts to amble out, Boo follows. "Nice and slow. You'll see," Harp says. We start heading to the street as a car zooms by.

"We going out there?" I say.

What is he thinking? I seen what happened the last time a horse was in the street.

"It's cool," he says. "We just gonna take a little neighborhood tour on the way to the Speedway. I'll take the quiet streets."

Next thing I know, we out in the streets. The horse hoofs is making a loud clip-clop noise on the brick road. Boo catches his hoof a coupla times on a brick, but he don't trip. I keep my eyes out for any runaway plastic bags.

Jamaica Bob comes out of one of the houses and gives a holler. "There they are: the champion and the protégé. You going to let him race today?"

Harper laughs. "Who, Lightning or Coltrane?"

Bob rubs his hands together. "Well, I know Lightning is running. Big Dee's in the hunt today."

Harp shakes his head. "The only thing Big Dee

is hunting is his next Big Mac. So maybe I'll give Coltrane a shot."

"Uh, I don't *think* so," I say.

Bob waves as he gets into his truck. "Yeah, well, as long as Harp races first. I'm planning to double my money today so I can pay that feed bill. Don't let me down!"

Harper waves as he drives away. We ride on, but his mind seem to be somewhere else.

We amble down Chester Avenue and turn down another street. I see Smush sitting on a stoop.

He holds up a fist. "Cuz! You still here? Don't let my uncle ride you too hard. I used to clean out them stables too, and let me tell you—"

But Harper's in no mood. "Smush, your daddy know you still a corner boy?"

Smush's smile disappears.

Harper gives him a look. "Maybe if you hung around the stable like you used to, you wouldn't be getting hassled all the time by the cops."

Smush waves him off. "I don't do that no more, Uncle Harp. I told you."

I can see Harp ain't buying it. "That's not what I hear, Smush. I better not see you out there, or I'll kick your butt back to the stables and you'll be working for me 24/7. You hear?"

"Yes, sir . . ." he mutters, then sits there silently as we ride by.

We pass a big ol' mural someone painted on the side of a building. It shows a street called Horseman Way and has all the riders hanging out on their horses. It's like a shot of the Old West, except instead of country, you got city, and instead of white folk, you got black cowboys.

I look closely and see Tex and Harper in the background.

"Is that *you* up there?" I ask.

He nods. "Yeah, that was from back when we must've had four hundred horsemen around here. But most of the stables been closed down by the City over the last few years. We one of the last ones in Philly to survive. There's probably less than eighty urban riders around here now, and most of them is struggling to find a place to put their horses. There might not be any of us left soon, if things keep going the way they are."

I think about what Jamaica Bob said yesterday. "Bob says the end is coming for all of you."

He grunts. "Maybe ten years from now, someone will pass this mural and think it's just a painting instead of a way of life."

FIFTEEN

We go a few more blocks. Folks pass us in the streets, smiling, waving. A car pulls alongside and a little girl says to me, "Are you a cowboy?"

I shake my head, but Harper says, "Yep, and we gonna race today!"

A block later, a group of kids come out, all asking for rides. He stops and gets off the horse.

"Who wants to ride?" he asks.

All their hands shoot up. He leans down to a coupla girls who look like sisters. "You wanna ride?"

They nod their heads. He lifts them up onto Lightning and starts guiding them gently, talking them through it. He seem like he got a way with kids. So how come he wasn't that way with me? I think of the first time I saw him with that gun, and he actin' so much nicer now.

For a half hour, we give rides. He even starts putting kids up on Boo with me and leading both horses around. They start asking me questions, and I answer what I can. One kid with a ol'-school Afro and gold necklace that says *CJ* on it asks why my horse don't got no bling. I don't know what he's talking about until he points to Lightning and I notice he got little shiny things braided in his mane and hanging off the saddle.

I ask Harp about that, and he says every rider tries to make his horse special, kinda like trickin' out a car. I look at Boo, and he ain't got nothin'.

Then I remember Mama's bracelet in my pocket. I ask this kid CJ if he knows how to tie a knot. He nods, and I give him the bracelet. He ties it onto Boo's hair and smiles. Bling.

CJ and them kids is looking at us like we rap stars who just stopped and gave them a ride in a limo. They all ready to race—"I can beat you!" CJ already saying, even though he can barely stay in the saddle.

Harper says they're all like that—ready to throw down before they can walk. They're all about speed and who can go fastest . . . until they grow older and get interested in girls, then they're all about *that*. "A girl beats a horse any day," he says, and laughs.

We show 'em a good time, but after a while, Harp looks at his watch.

"Gotta go!" he says, cutting them off. "Gotta earn my keep. But you all come down to Chester Avenue and you can learn to ride for real. How's that sound?"

They all jump up and down, asking if they can come tomorrow. Harp smiles and says he'll be there. On the way out, I see CJ still watching us.

"Save one kid by getting them into horses and it's all worth it," Harp says to me. He got a strange look in his eyes that makes me think maybe he was one of them kids that Tex took in a long time ago. "You never know what someone will do with his life once he finds himself."

We ride a little farther, past a few pretty girls sitting on a stoop. "Morning, ladies," he calls out.

I nod too.

Philly girls is hot. They all smile and wave, and I remember how much girls like horses. *Man, is this all I need to get a fine one like that?*

We ride on, and I'm starting to like this. It still feels weird up here, but I can't help but think what it woulda been like if I grew up this way. Would I be like Harper, all into horses, working in the stables every day, keeping busy? How would it be growing up with him and not Mama? Would we do more man stuff, being cowboys and hanging with the guys? Would it be any better? Or would I just end up like Smush, some corner boy with a mouth on him?

SIXTEEN

We turn a corner and at the end of the street, I can see it: the park. After a few minutes, we leave the city behind us, and it's like we in the country all of a sudden. Trees everywhere. I can hear the wind blowing on the leaves as we make our way across the grass.

We pass a swimming pool with a bunch of kids in it. Some of 'em see the horses and press their faces up against the chain-link fence to get a look. We mosey down a trail, past some tennis courts. The sound of the city is far off in the distance. I can hear birds chirping, something I ain't heard in a long time.

I ease up, feel okay on Boo's back. Harp tells me Fairmount Park is one of the biggest parks in America — so big, you can even get lost in it. We ride, and for a good while I can't see no buildings no more, only trees. We could be anywhere, a thousand miles from the city. I ain't never seen so much trees and stuff.

Then I hear it. Laughing, music, cheering . . . and a rumble. We come out through some trees into a clearing, and I see what the rumbling is: two horses racing toward us faster than I ever thought a horse could go. They fly by us, two young guys, hootin' it up, and one of 'em raises his fist like he won.

I look down the other way, and all the guys is there — Tex, Bob, and then some — cheering, cursing, paying off money. Behind them is a bunch of cars, some women sitting on beach chairs with coolers and stuff, a few kids running around chasing each other.

"This is it. The Speedway," Harp says.

"*This* is the Speedway? It's just a strip of grass in a park."

"You was expecting Churchill Downs? This is where the real deal is."

I shrug. "Whatever you say."

He laughs at me. "Boy, what do you know? Black horse trainers started racing retired Thoroughbreds here a hundred years ago. How do you think the Chester Avenue tradition got started?"

The two racers come galloping up to us. "Harper! We ain't seen you around here for a while. So it's true, you gonna race?"

I look at Harper, who scratches his head, glancing over at the crowd across the way. "Maybe. What're they saying?"

The guy who won smiles. "Big Dee saying you too old. Past your prime. And that Lightning's racing days are over and done."

"Who's racing his horse?"

They look at each other. "You don't know? Carmelo."

Harper's face changes, gets all grim.

"Who's Carmelo?" I ask.

Harper don't answer, so one of the guys pipes in.

"Carmelo is the new sheriff out here. You're nobody if you don't beat Carmelo. And nobody beats Carmelo."

"I beat him," Harp says.

The guys look at each other. "Yeah, Harp, but that was a long time ago. Last time, he whupped your—"

Harp raises his hand. "He cheated. Cut me off. It's all on video."

The guys look at each other, unsure.

Harp shrugs. "Hey, you wanna bet against me, go ahead. Just make sure it's money you don't need anymore, because you ain't gonna be keeping it."

He turns and ambles toward the starting line, Boo an' me following along. When the other guys see him, a cheer goes up.

I see Big Dee dressed in a bright-red Sixers jacket and cap and big ol' shades. "Well, well, well. Look who it is, the Lone Ranger and Tonto," he says, grinning.

I have no idea what he talking about.

He looks at me. "You his son, right?"

I nod.

"That's too bad. I hope you don't mind if my horse puts your daddy to shame. Hate to ruin his rep in front of you and all."

I see Harp roll his eyes.

I shrug. "Don't make no difference to me." I'm joking, but Harp gives me a look out of the corner of his eye.

"He's coming!" someone shouts. He ain't talking about Harper, 'cause heads turn away from us and the crowd splits apart as some slick-looking dude with gold-rimmed shades and a black head wrap rides in.

I don't know nothing about horses, but that horse looks ripped, like it's built for speed. The guy rides right up to us, but ignores me.

"You came back for more?" he says to Harp.

"I came back for a legit race, Carmelo. You gonna keep in your lane?"

"Always do, Harp. You got Lightning hopped up on them special 'vitamins'?"

Harper turns and spits. "This horse is one-hundred percent natural. Always has been, always will be."

They stare each other down like I seen fighters do before a boxing match. Finally, Jamaica Bob interrupts.

"Well, guys, you heard it. It's the rematch of the century! Now, who's gonna put their money where their mouth is?"

Suddenly, there's like a rush, and everyone's holding out cash as Bob takes it and writes it down in a little black book.

"This one's even odds. Quarter-mile sprint. I don't know who's gonna win, but it's gonna be good, that's fer sure."

He turns to Harper and winks. Harper breaks off his stare and leans down to Bob. "If I don't win, we'll both have to pack our bags."

He hands me the rope attached to my saddle. "Tie Boo up to that tree there. Then you can watch with Bob."

I look at Carmelo, acting all cocky. "You gonna win this?" I ask Harp.

"Why, what's it to you?"

I reach in my pocket. "I got ten bucks to bet. You gonna win?"

He smiles, nods. "Go make some money, son," he says, taking his cowboy hat and plopping it on my head.

I ain't never wore no cowboy hat before. "Don't you need this to race?" I ask. But he's already galloping off to the starting line.

I tilt my hat so I'll look all fly. Then I try to steer Boo over to the tree, but suddenly, he don't wanna move. "Giddyup!" I yell.

Nothing. Boo just stuck to the ground. Them kids who was washing horses earlier is laughing at us, having a good ol' time.

Finally, I gotta get off and pull him by his rope.

Carmelo passes by, shaking his head, and mutters, "You don't deserve to wear that hat."

I give him the evil eye. I sure hope Harper puts him and Big Dee to shame.

SEVENTEEN

I try not to look at the guys as I tie Boo to the tree. "Why you gotta make me look bad, Boo?"

He looks at me all sorry. Dumb horse. But then he bows his head and waits for me to pet him. I roll my eyes but end up petting his neck while he chews on the grass, and he seem like a dog you can't help but love, even if he trouble sometimes.

I make my bet. One of the little kids stares at me wide-eyed as I hand over my cash. "What? That's how I roll. I'm a playa, understand?"

He giggles at the clothes I slept in. "You ain't got no money!"

I chase him off. "Punk. You'll see." He's still laughing at me.

At the starting line, Harp and Lightning is chomping at the bit. Carmelo and Rocket trot over. I can see the horses don't like each other neither, nipping at each other like a coupla pit bulls looking for a fight. Bad blood.

A older woman with a fake blond wig on walks out with a red bandanna in her hand. The guys all whistle, and she makes a face, like, *Ain't I pretty?* even though she ain't really. She gets to a spot about twenty feet in front of the horses but off to the side.

"Ready?" She waves the flag around.

"I'm always ready, honey!" someone shouts out to laughs.

"Set!"

Harp and Carmelo line up their horses like they struggling to hold 'em back.

"GO!"

Rocket bolts, but Lightning seem to be stuck in neutral, like there's an invisible wall in front of him. Harper don't panic, though. After a beat, he yells, and Lightning, well . . . it's like he *explodes* outta there. He takes off and the ground is shaking and he goes after Rocket. I can't believe my eyes, but somehow Lightning is catching up to him! The guys is going crazy, yelling and climbing over each other. Even I'm jumping up and down. Finally, Lightning and Rocket is running side by side and I swear, I see Harper look over and nod, like, *See ya later,* and he shoots past Carmelo!

Now everyone really goin' crazy and that woman is jumping up and down laughing and Harper passes the spot where we came in and holds up his arms and points to the sky.

I jump in the air and yell, *"Yes!"* Some of the guys is on their knees pounding the ground like they can't believe what they just saw neither. The kids is running around, whooping it up.

Jamaica Bob yells out, "The champ is back!"

Big Dee just stands there stewing, then heads over to his truck. Money changes hands, and the ones who bet on Harp is really happy.

"Now, *that* was a race!" I hear Tex say. "Just like the old days!"

I see Harper trotting back, sitting up in the saddle, all smiles. Carmelo's still down at the other end, looking away from us like he trying to figure out what happened.

Bob hands me a twenty-dollar bill. "Looks like you made a good bet," he says.

Everyone rushes around Harper as he gets off Lightning and pats him on the back.

"Now, that's how it's done!" he says, all proud. "Where's Big Dee?"

Bob points to the truck where Big Dee is sitting behind his shades. Harp nods, and Dee nods back. He don't look too happy.

Someone turns up the music. It's that song "Celebration," and the guys start dancing and screaming for Big Dee's benefit. *"Ceeeelebrate good times, come on!"* Even I get into it. Big Dee just shakes his big head. When Carmelo rides up to his truck, they have a few words, and they don't look like good ones.

The song ends, and the woman hands Harper a Coke. He gulps it down, then says, "Victory sure do taste sweet!"

I go up to him and hold out the twenty. "What's that for?" he asks.

"That's my winnings. I kinda borrowed it yesterday."

He don't seem to mind. "Keep it. I got my own winnings coming."

Jamaica Bob slaps Harp on the back and hands him a small stack of bills. "To the victor go the spoils!"

Harper grins and pockets the cash without counting it.

"Your old man ain't so old now, is he?" Bob asks me.

Looking at Harp all happy, he do seem younger.

Bob takes the hat offa my head and plops it back on Harper. "Your daddy is a legend around here. Nobody's won more races, even though he only races a few times a year these days."

Harp acts all modest. "Well, maybe I'll come outta retirement for this kinda cash."

He sees Carmelo, but before he heads over, he leans down toward me. "You know, if you stick around, you might learn a thing or two. You could follow in my footsteps, be a racer."

I look at all the love he getting and think that might be all right, but I just nod. I watch him go up to Carmelo and expect to see him put that punk in his place, but instead he says something quiet and they hug.

Word musta got out, because on the way home, we run into a block party and it seem like everyone's on the street or hanging out their windows saying nice things to him. I can see it makes Harper feel good to be out among the people, treating him like a real neighborhood hero or something. He gets held up by some friends, but nobody seem to notice me so much, mostly 'cause he don't introduce me. I end up waiting around for him, and even though some lady gives me a drink to pass the time with, I don't know nobody here, so I wanna leave. Finally, after about a half hour, he sees me and nods and we head on back.

"Been a while since I seen a lot of those folks. Nice party, wasn't it?" he asks.

I shrug and ignore him.

When we get to the stables, Tex and Jamaica Bob is already there. I get off Boo, and Bob takes him back into the stable. Harp calls Tex over and hands the stack of bills to him.

"Use this to take care of that dead horse. The meat vendors won't take him now, but see that the body is disposed of proper-like."

Tex glances at the money. "But this is your winnings, son."

"Yep. And we can't afford to have a dead horse around here, can we? Mrs. Elders can't afford to do nothing, so there it is."

Tex wanders off, counting the cash. "Too bad. Coulda bought some nice feed with this."

Harp looks down at me, then holds out his hand.

"What?" I say.

I think he wants me to shake it, but all he say is, "You hungry?"

I gotta admit I am. "Maybe."

"Well, come on, then."

I put out my hand, and he grabs it and swings me up onto Lightning like we in a rodeo. I don't know how he did that, but he nods like it ain't no big thing.

"Hold on," he says.

He puts my arms around him as we trot back out onto the street. I can feel the warmth from his back and then I realize, this is the first time I ever hugged my daddy.

EIGHTEEN

Harp asks me if I ever had a Philly cheesesteak. I don't know much, but I know steak, and it ain't made of cheese. But I seen a place in Detroit called Philly's Cheesesteak, so I guess it's not a joke.

He takes me to this place around the corner, and we stand in line in front of this little shack. He talks to the guy and then turns around with two gigantic sandwiches. "Gotta have the complete Philly experience."

We sitting on the curb, and even though this sandwich got a weird name, I dig in . . . and it's *sooo* good! Where I'm from, we got Coney dogs and deep-dish pizza. But I ain't had nothing like this.

Both of us is chowing down when a cop car pulls up in front of us. The window rolls down, and this black cop with a shaved head stares at us through his mirrored glasses.

"That your horse?" he asks, looking at Lightning, who's tied up to a sign.

Harper don't even look over, acts all innocent. "That isn't my horse, Officer," he says.

Cop seem to know he lying, and I'm thinking maybe you can't ride a horse on the streets.

"Heard you did a little racing down at the Speedway this morning."

Harp looks up and gives him major 'tude. "Yeah, and what's it to you, *pig*?"

I think now is as good a time as any to start running, but Harper grabs my sleeve and holds on.

The cop shakes his head. "You have any idea how fast you were going in that race? Because I got a good mind to give you . . . a *speeding violation!*"

With that, he whips off his shades and grins like a fool. Harper starts laughing, slapping his leg and elbowing me, and I get it now, they friends. He reaches out and gives the cop a fist bump.

"So where were *you*?" Harper says. "I coulda used that speed gun, 'cause Lightning was flying for sure."

The cop sighs. "Yeah, so I heard. Next time you crawl outta that hole you call a stable, let me know and I'll be there. Last time I heard you raced was a while back."

Harp wipes his mouth on his sleeve. "Yeah, yeah. So how come you don't ride that horse of yours our way no more?"

The cop shrugs. "Had to move him to Jersey. That was the only place that had room after they closed the Bunker stables. But if you up for a race, I could make that trip. . . ." He smiles, like he knows that ain't never gonna happen.

His radio goes off, and he responds. "Gotta go, Harp. North Philly can't last two minutes without something bad going down. Duty calls."

"Later days, pig!" Harper laughs. "I mean, Leroy!"

Leroy laughs, turns on his flashing lights, then hits the road, siren blaring.

Harper watches him go and says, "Good guy, that Leroy. We used to ride a lot back in the day."

I ask how he knows a cop, and he says riding brings together all kind of folks: electricians, trashmen, bus drivers, teachers, mailmen, even cops.

"So what is your job? What do you do?" I ask him.

He looks at his feet. "Survive," he says, all grim. "Survive."

NINETEEN

On the way back to his house, Harp tells me he done just about everything. Used to work at the racetrack, Philadelphia Park, as a training assistant. But since he was laid off, he been in janitorial, construction, fast food, newspaper delivery, even dug graves at a cemetery once. He still takes any stable work he can get, but spends most of his time caring for the horses on Chester Avenue.

"They pay you for that?"

He laughs. "Nah, *we* pay the stables. It's like a co-op—we all pitch in and help, but we gotta pay for everything too. You know how much it costs to feed a horse?"

I shrug, but Harp ain't even looking.

"I can barely hold on," he says to no one. "And now I got you to think about too."

We ride up to his place in silence. The sky is getting dark, some clouds coming in.

"Looks like rain. Might help cool things off," he says.

We get to his front door, and he glances back at me.

"You coming in? Or maybe you like staying at the Ritz better."

"I guess I'll come in," I say.

He nods, then lowers me offa Lightning before climbing down himself.

"Look, I been around on this earth a bit, and one thing I know is, life ain't fair. You get dealt the hand you get dealt and you get on with it. So if you wanna run away, be my guest. I understand. I was your age once." He sees me smirk. "Yeah, go ahead and laugh. All I'm saying is, if you wanna stay . . . we can try and make it work."

I nod. "We'll see."

I take a step, then ask, "Maybe we can call Mama again?"

Harper sighs, looks doubtful. "Wait a few days. . . . Let things simmer. But don't get your hopes up."

He leads Lightning up the stoop past me and ducks into the house, the hoofs echoing on the wood floor. Harper pulls him into the hole in the wall, and I stand in the doorway and think about Mama and what she doing alone in her apartment. Now that I got people all around me, it makes me wonder if she feels all lonely now. Is she sitting by the window, hatin' on herself for leaving me here? Or maybe she at some club thinking she got her life back now.

I blink. Feel water on me. It's starting to rain. Harper's standing inside looking at me.

"You just gonna stand there or you coming in?"

I step inside.

"I wanna play you something," he says.

I sit down on the one chair in the room. He goes over to a record player sitting on a wood box, digs through a pile a records, and pulls one out. They look like giant black CDs. He puts it on.

This horn comes on, loud and strong. Then it settles and a drum and bass join in. It's moody and dark, like I'm feeling.

"That's John Coltrane, your namesake," Harp says. "He lived around here, ya know. A Philly man."

He sits on the floor, his back against the wall, and closes his eyes. I lean back and let the music take over. I never really listened to jazz before. Maybe now

TWENTY

When I wake, I don't know where I am. Then it dawns on me that I'm in Harper's bed upstairs.

How'd I get up here? I can't remember.

Harper ain't around. I sit up and slowly the world comes to my head. It's day outside but dark, 'cause I can still hear the rain falling on the roof. There is some kinda commotion going on outside, and I go to the window to check it out. The rain is coming down harder than I seen in a long time. I hear a buncha noise and look down to the street in front of us.

Jamaica Bob has his truck pulled up, and he and Harper is loading stuff into the pickup—wood, hammers, and stuff. They must be crazy doing this in the pouring rain. I go to the top of the stairs. Harper comes back in to grab some rope. He already soaked and the day's just starting.

"Why you working in the rain?" I ask.

He looks at me, shakes his head. "Stay here."

He heads back into the downpour. I go downstairs and see Jamaica Bob grabbing a toolbox outta Lightning's room.

"What happened?" I ask.

"Storm tore a hole in the Ritz. Gotta move some horses and try to patch that roof before it gets worse."

"Is Boo okay?"

He grimaces. "He got out in time, but he's a little . . ."

"What?" I ask.

"Well, you know. He's a bit out of control."

"I'm coming with you," I say, looking for my shoes.

Bob shakes his head. "Harper wants you to stay here. Says you'll just get in the way."

He shuts the door behind him as he leaves. I stare at the doorknob, thinking of Boo, and getting madder by the minute. *Get in the way? What am I, a baby?* If helping Boo means getting in the way, then the heck with Harper.

I get dressed. Outside, it's really pouring now. From the window, I can see a small river moving through the street. I find a old rain poncho in the closet, but my shoes ain't gonna help me none. I look by the door and there's them cowboy boots Harper gave me.

Better than nothing.

It take me five minutes to figure out how to get them dag boots on my feet. I pull and pull and finally, I get my foot all the way in.

I stand up and I feel five inches taller. It's kinda weird walking around in these things. They squeeze on my toes. They sound loud walking on the wood floors. But they'll do.

Next thing I know, I'm trudging through the rain. The only plus is it ain't cold out. I keep moving, crossing the street where I can and getting out the way of passing cars so I don't get drowned by a wave.

When I get to the stable, it looks like a war zone. It's a real mess—mud everywhere. A lot of guys, some I never seen before, is moving horses, hauling wood, soaked to the bone. Must be twenty of 'em come out to help. I head over to the Ritz, and the second I walk in, I see it: a huge hole opened up over Boo's stall.

I panic. "Where's Boo?"

Harper spots me and looks pissed. "Go home. He's okay. Damn thing busted out before it all fell down. Lucky he ran into the corral. Tex is trying to calm him."

The last thing I'm gonna do is go home now. I head back out to the corral. Boo is running in circles, and Tex and another guy is trying to rope him.

"Boo!" I shout.

Tex sees me. "Stay out, kid. He's spooked."

The rain is coming down so hard, I can barely see. My feet is sinking into the mud, so I scramble up onto the fence around the corral. Boo's actin' crazy, the whites of his eyes wide and a kind of foam coming out his mouth. Tex tries to calm him, but Boo jumps every time he gets near and just keeps running in circles.

Tex and the other guy slowly corner him against the fence, and I see Boo's hoofs getting itchy like he gonna bust right out. But then a funny thing happens.

Just when I thought he was gonna run over Tex, Boo suddenly sees me sitting on the fence and stops. Just plain stops and stares at me. It's spooky, like he trying to speak to me through mind talk or something. He looking at me, and I swear, it seem like all his fear disappears.

Tex slowly clumps his way through the mud and gets a rope on Boo. Boo don't fight back but starts moving closer to me, dragging Tex with him. I'm kinda scared, but I reach out 'cause it looks like he wants me to pet his head since we on the same level.

Boo stands there staring at me, totally calm as my

hand touches his mane. And it's like everything stops; all the craziness disappears. It's just me and Boo.

Tex laughs. "That is the darndest thing I ever saw. I think you got a friend."

I don't know if he talking to me or Boo, but I don't argue. After a few minutes, I let Tex lead Boo out the corral to a little overhang thing in the side yard. He ties him up and says, "Stay, Boo."

I ask, "You just gonna leave him out here?"

Tex looks over at the Ritz. "Got to. No place to put him until we get that roof closed up. He'll be okay."

Boo looks like them homeless guys you see on street benches, all dirty and scruffy, hair going every which way. At least he outta the rain.

I run into the clubhouse and find a coupla carrots in Tex's stash. When Boo sees me with them, he gets all excited, tugging on his rope. I hold them out, and he chomps them one at a time. I pet him on his neck as he chews away. He calms down and starts chewing slower, just looking at me. I tell him he be all right. I think he believes me.

I'm standing next to him when he finishes, and then he moves his head until it's resting against mine. We just stand there, listening to the rain fall on the metal roof over us.

TWENTY-ONE

I hear a shout. The wind kicks up, and someone jumps off the ladder that was going up to the roof of the Ritz.

Harper.

A blue tarp up top whips about in the wind. I hear him shout to Jamaica Bob, "That roof ain't gonna hold me. I'm too heavy to get up there."

Bob's trying to look up into the rain and wind. "We can't fix it till this rain stops! But we got to get that tarp tied down."

Suddenly my mouth opens. "I can climb up there."

Harper, Tex, and Bob all turn and look at me. They wouldn'ta been more surprised if Boo had spoken up. I don't know why I opened my big mouth. Maybe I was just trying to show Harper I ain't totally useless.

But they don't say no.

Bob shrugs. "Kid might be light enough. We could tie a rope to him."

I can see Harper thinking hard, and it feels like maybe he don't want me to get hurt. But then he asks me, "Can you climb?"

I think, *Yeah, I can climb. I hopped enough fences in my time. I can climb up onto a old barn.*

I nod.

Next thing I know, Harper is tying a rope to my waist. Tex stands there, holding up the ladder leading to the broken roof. The blue tarp whips about, the rope ties flying in the wind.

Harper leans in close. "If you feel like you're falling, jump. I'll catch ya."

I give him a look, like, *Yeah, right,* but it's better having him down here than not.

I grab on to the metal ladder. It's cold to my hands. I feel like one of them fire-rescue guys, only there ain't no flames.

Bob give me a thumbs-up, but he starting to look

worried. He trades words with Harper, who seem even more worried. They stare at the tarp whipping around and shake their heads. I know they gonna change their minds, so I start climbing before they can say anything.

About halfway up, I feel the rope tugging on me. Harp is yelling something, but I can't hear him 'cause the rain and the wind is so loud. I wave him off and keep going.

The ladder is shaking from the gusts. I hold on tight, afraid I'm just gonna slip off. The rain keep blowing in my eyes and blinding me. Them cowboy boots I'm wearing got no grip, so they keep slipping off the ladder too. Then there's the tarp and the ropes, snapping around my head like whips. I think one of 'em might cut my head off.

What was I thinking?

I look back down. Everyone's staring at me. But I don't wanna wuss out.

Once I get up to the edge of the roof, I can see why Harp jumped. The hole looks like someone dropped a car through it. I look down into the void and see Boo's stall, crushed by the missing piece of roof. Man.

What's left up there seem real rickety. I can hear it squealing as it moves around in the wind. A big gust hits me, and I almost lose it—grab on with all my might and shut my eyes tight. When they open again, I can see the three guys holding the ladder still and Harper waving me back down.

I look away. I can see the lay of the land from up here. The whole place is a mess, like it's been hit by a tornado or something. But the worst thing is seeing that dead horse lying there in the mud—this is the tarp they was using to cover it.

I take a deep breath and pray for the wind to die down for a second. When it does, I take the last three steps and then I'm up on top.

I keep my eye on the ropes whizzing around me. I use to catch flies all the time, so I pretend they just a couple a of bugs buzzing around my head. The first time I reach for one, I almost fall off. I end up on my stomach looking down into the darkness. My mind goes blank, and I hold on like my hands is made of glue. But just as I start thinking of jumping, one of them ropes hits me in the head and I snag it, wrapping it around my arm.

Now what? I see Harper pointing to something. I follow his finger and see a wood beam sticking out from the edge of the building. He making motions like I should tie it around that beam. The only problem is I got to crawl along the edge of this roof about fifteen feet to get to it.

With the rain and the wind and all the noise and spooked horses and guys shouting . . . somehow I just start moving. The building creaks and squeals; pieces fall off left and right. But all of a sudden I'm there. I just have to hold on with my legs, reach down, and pull that rope tight around the beam till the tarp stops flapping about and lays down over that hole. I don't know how to tie no knot, so I just wrap it and crisscross it till it sticks.

I hear a cheer go up and them guys down below is all smiles. And suddenly, I don't feel scared no more.

I make my way backwards to the ladder. When I get there, the other rope is just lying there, like a present or something. I grab it and look down, where they waving me back. The rope seem long enough, so I just pull it down with me. The ladder don't seem as rickety going down.

When I get back to earth, they all treat me like I had just won one of them races. All slaps on the back and guys saying, "Way to go" and stuff. Even Harper has a different look in his eyes.

For the first time since I got here, I feel all right.

TWENTY-TWO

They tie that rope nice and tight around a post, and looking into the barn, I can see the blue tarp has stopped the rain for now. Hopefully, it'll clear up and they can fix it for real tomorrow.

In the meantime, we all head back to the clubhouse to get out of the storm. When the door opens . . . man, something smells *good*.

Some of the old-time cowboys been cooking up something tasty, and we have us a big ol' party. There must be thirty guys in here now, and the funny thing is, they all treatin' me like I'm no different than them. We eat and drink (well, I don't have no beer, but they brought out root beer for me) and complain about the craziness of this storm, an' how global warming is making the weather all backwards.

When things get good and toasty, Tex starts telling us some of his stories from the olden days, back when he was a rodeo star in Texas (that's why they call him Tex, duh), one of the first black cowboys to make his mark on the circuit. Everyone says he was the best in his day, but he says his daddy and granddaddy was even better.

"Back in them days, they used to roam the open country, herding cattle on the Chisholm Trail." The guys nod, like that's something they heard about the Old West.

"What's so special 'bout that?" I ask.

Tex's eyes get all dreamy. "That was back when you could ride for days on end without seeing a city. Just open land as far as the eye could see — no fences, no roads. They slept under the stars, bathed in the river, and when they was hungry, they just shot a rabbit and ate it!"

"I hope they cooked it first," I say, and they all bust up like I said something funny. I can't really imagine living that way. Seem like my whole life, everywhere I looked was city — walls, freeways, and buildings. I hardly ever seen a open stretch of land with no cement on it.

"That was back when the Cowboy Way meant

something. Ain't that right, Tex?" Harp asks. Tex nods in agreement.

"What's the Cowboy Way?" I ask.

Harper puts down his drink and glances at everyone around him. The old guys smile like they know; some of the younger ones just shrug. "The Cowboy Way started because, back in the day, you couldn't trust the law."

"Still can't," Tex pipes in.

"Law was under the rule of the land barons. The sheriffs did what barons said and ignored the will of the people. So the cowboys had to take on their own brand of justice—cowboy justice. All that John Wayne stuff—you know, you can live outside the law as long as you're honest and live by the code. Don't steal nobody's cattle or their women. Treat your horse like it was your best friend, because sometimes that's all you got. Most important, trust and believe in your guys and always have their back when they need you."

The old-timers is nodding, saying *Amen* and *You got that right.*

"The Cowboy Way is, no matter what, never ever give up fighting when the chips are down. Real cowboys *never* give up," Harp says, staring me down like he wants me to believe that.

I look around, and it's like one big family, everyone helping out and watching out for each other. And it feels like Harp now wants me there too.

"Ain't nothing changed," says Jamaica Bob. "Cowboys still fighting to protect their ways in land wars where the bosses are trying to run 'em out. Only difference now is, the Chisholm Trail is a freeway today. We got to stick to our ways so that the young people have a safe place in this world, a place where the old values still count."

He raises his bottle, and even the younger guys yell out in agreement. We all raise our bottles too, and looking around at all these cowboys makes me feel like we in the Old West still.

TWENTY-THREE

Once we back in the house, I stare out the window, thinking what would it be like to stay here and live the Cowboy Way. Hanging out with all of them, that might be all right. I could learn to ride, maybe teach other kids how to work at the stables, and I wouldn't have to worry about school no more. I could just be a cowboy 'cause if you a cowboy, you do as you feel, not as you're told.

"You don't have to sleep in the closet if you don't want to."

I turn and see Harper staring at me. He scratches his head and says, "If you want to, you can sleep in my bed."

"With you?" I ask.

He laughs. "Yeah, with me. I ain't sleeping in the closet!"

I laugh. Anything is better than that closet.

That night, though, I can't sleep. I lay there listening to Harper snore. Off in the distance I hear a gunshot, thumpin' car music, and choppers in the air. I keep thinking about Mama and when she gonna show up and take me back so I can start summer school. But she seem farther away than ever.

I don't remember falling asleep, but Boo musta still been on my mind 'cause I had this dream where I was riding him along the Chisholm Trail. We was heading up to Detroit, rustling cattle and all. Harp and Tex and Jamaica Bob was there too. There was no cities, no loud cars, no gunshots. Only wide-open forever, as far as I could see. We sat around a fire at night, eating beans and such and listening to a cowboy named John Coltrane play his sax (I said it was a dream). The last thing I remember was coming to the end of the trail and seeing a big city off in the distance. Harper says to me, "There it is. That's where your mama's at." But I don't remember riding off to it.

• • •

When I wake up, it's still early. The clock says five thirty, and Harper's dead asleep. I get up and look out the window. The rain has finally stopped, but everything feels like it's drenched to the bone. I can see the Ritz-Carlton from here. That blue tarp, which I almost killed myself over, blew loose and is drooping down into the hole in the roof.

Dag. I think of Boo again and suddenly feel like going to see how he holding up. I find my boots and coat and sneak out without waking Harper. I shush Lightning as I walk past. He ignores me.

Outside, the stoop leads right into a lake. The whole street is flooded. The water come up to the middle of my boots as I move slowly through it, so's not to get mud down into my socks. Nobody's out yet, and the place seem eerie quiet.

Where there ain't water, there's mud, like it just washed everything from the vacant lots onto the streets. What a mess. I climb the fence over into the stables and immediately spot Boo. He musta been rolling around in muck and who knows what, 'cause his fur all ruffled up and covered in mud.

Poor Boo. He look like a Skid Row horse or something awful. But he brightens up when he sees me. I pet him on the head, and he seem okay—same ol' Boo. Just needs a bath is all. I grab some hay and feed him. I can see some of the other horses in the corral all muddy like Boo, but they don't seem to mind. At least it looks like no more rain. Hopefully we can get this place all cleaned up soon enough.

TWENTY-FOUR

I'm brushing down Boo when I see three black vans pull up in front of the stable and come skidding to a halt. A chill shoots down my neck and I think, *This ain't right.*

Suddenly, about twenty guys in blue Windbreakers jump out and swarm the stables like ants, trekking through the mud and taking pictures and video of everything they see. *What the heck is going on?* One thing's for sure—Harper's *not* gonna be happy.

I stand frozen to the ground, thinking, *If I move, they'll pounce on me too.* They just pass by me like I'm invisible, whistling to each other every time they find something that's broken down or beat up 'cause of the storm.

Tex pokes his head out the clubhouse, his big ol' glasses peering out as he ties his robe up. But he looks as confused as I am. Maybe he thinks he drank too much last night, 'cause he laughing for some reason. It all seem too crazy.

A overweight white man in a dark suit comes over to him, waving a piece of paper and saying he got a court order to shut us down. Tex just stares at him, shaking his head. I don't like this guy neither. Guys in suits make me feel all jumpy. I think they from the City 'cause all the other dudes got *Dept. of License and Inspection* on their jackets.

But all Tex do is turn and walk away toward the street. He waving the guy off like he a fly or something. The guy follows him around the corner.

I got no idea what to do. Them dudes seem all nervous, like they know a battle's coming. Sure enough, I hear a commotion coming from the street. People is yelling and the other City dudes rush back to the front. Then I know—Harper's here.

When I get to the gate, I see Harper going face-to-face with the man in the suit. The suit is telling him the stables is unsanitary (he pointing at the huge pile of crap) and the horses is in danger and he never seen nothing like this and he gonna shut us down.

I know what's coming now, 'cause telling Harp he a danger to these animals is like insulting his mama. It's a throwdown, and one he ain't gonna stand for.

Six or seven of the other riders come running from down the street. Tex, Jamaica Bob, and the Malcolm X cowboys all got Harper's back—everyone's yelling at the suit, and things is gettin' crazy. I see some of the neighbors looking out their windows, some shaking their heads like they saying, *'Bout time,* others just lookin' sad. Some kids come out in their pajamas, looking all scared and confused.

I gotta climb on the fence so I can see what's happening. About six cops have showed up like they was expecting this, and they all crowd around Harper too. The yelling is intense, and the cops take out their clubs, ready for action. Our guys push back, and it looks like there's gonna be a fight and I think, *This is it!*

But then the suit with the paper yells out, "Just read it!"

Harper grinds his teeth, then holds up his hand, and the yelling dies down. I can see his jaw clenching from here. He reading the court order, shaking his head. The other neighborhood guys is looking over his shoulder. I hear them mutter, *It's a setup. They framed us. They can't do this!*

Then I spot one of them dudes in the Windbreakers coming from behind the corral where the giant pile of you-know-what is. He a white dude, but he looks super white now, like he seen a ghost. He starts talking to the suit and pointing back to the pile, which is steaming from all the rain and heat. And 'cause he so frantic and all, I'm pretty sure I know what they talking about.

That white dude just found the body of the dead horse.

Man. I see Harper bow his head and breathe slowly. When he gazes up at the sky, I see tears coming down his face, like he knows he ain't got no chance now. Maybe he seen it one too many times. Tex said the white man always wins in the end. Maybe he's right, 'cause even though it wasn't their fault, a dead body, no matter what, won't look good.

But that's not the worst thing. I move in closer, and I hear the suit say, "Due to the conditions of this facility, I'm going to have to confiscate the horses that look malnourished."

Harper mumbles, "What?"

But the suit has more to say. "The other horses will have to be cleared out and stabled somewhere else in the next twenty-four hours."

Tex gets in the man's face. "Why?"

The suit don't blink. "Because come eight o'clock tomorrow morning, our bulldozers will start to tear down these illegal facilities."

Tex is ready to kill the suit as he starts pointing out horses that they're gonna take. He walking around with some kinda horse "expert," acting like he picking out stuff to throw away for garbage pickup! One of the older kids in his pj's starts screaming when he takes his horse, Daisy.

Five or six of the other old heads in the 'hood come outta their houses, like they sensed a change in the wind or something. Even though it's early, they dressed with their cowboy hats and big belt buckles and boots. They make their way through the crowd and lay their hands on Harper's shoulders. They whisper in his ear. He pleading to the suit now, the fight all gone from him, the old heads holding him up. They all crying too, and they pretty tough guys.

I feel like taking out the suit right now, and I walk straight at him like I'm gonna do it too. But then I see him point at Boo, and my heart stops. I can't think straight. I see Boo looking all scared and alone, and suddenly, I know I got to do something before it's too late.

I run over and grab his rope, and a couple City guys come over and try to take him from me. They say things like, *It's all right. We're going to take care of him—make him all better.*

I say, "He ain't sick!" but it's like they can't hear me. "He just look scruffy 'cause of the storm!" I yell, but they act like he been starving and living on the street. Another guy who looks like a vet is checking him out, looking in Boo's mouth, but Boo don't like it and tries to bite him.

I see a horse truck back up, and then I get a bad feeling in my gut. Like if I let Boo go, he ain't never gonna come back. He'll disappear and won't ever see his friends again, won't ever get back home again. He'll end up in a strange place where nobody cares about him, and then when he turns his back, they'll kill him and make him into dog food. Or worse, he'll end up like that horse out back—dead and forgotten.

And that's when I freak. I kick one of the guys in

the leg, rip the rope outta his hands, and try to climb up on Boo so I can make a break for it. Problem is, Boo ain't wearing a saddle, and he buggin' out for sure. He jumping around, and the guys try to pull me off. Boo starts kicking, and I go flying off into the mud, smack on my back, the wind knocked outta me.

I fight to get my breath back, but when I look up, my heart stops—Boo is on his back legs, towering over me. He look like a giant, his hoofs scrambling in the air in slow motion right above me, and suddenly I know it's all over. Boo gonna stomp me into the mud, and that'll be it. I cover my eyes and wait for it, everyone yelling and Boo crying out—

Then I feel a hand grab me and pull me out the way. I open one eye and see it's Harper.

He standing between me and Boo, raising his arms up and doing that horse-whisper stuff I seen him do before. Boo backs up, and Harper with him like they in a dance. Then he lowers his hands and Boo slowly comes down and Harper reaches for the rope and he comes in and hugs Boo 'round the neck.

Boo looks at me, maybe wondering why I'm lying in the mud. Jamaica Bob helps me up as the City guys try to take Boo again. But Harper says to them, "Hold on, hold on." And he starts walking Boo past them.

At that moment, I think Harper's gonna save Boo and everything's gonna be all right. But then he turns toward the truck and pulls Boo right into the trailer!

He gonna give in? Just like that?

I get up and start running over, but Bob grabs me and whispers in my ear, "Let him go, son." *Has everyone gone crazy?* They load up maybe eight horses, and Harper just stands there, his back to me, holding that piece of paper. Bob got a iron grip and won't let go.

We watch the City guys finish up and in a few more minutes, they all gone, like it never happened.

TWENTY-FIVE

Nobody talks. Nobody moves. The neighbors disappear from their windows. I look down in the mud and see Mama's bracelet that was tied to Boo's mane. I run over to pick it up and hold it tight.

I can't see straight no more. My ears is ringing, my throat is all tight, and my stomach is on fire—it's like a volcano erupts in my head. When I see Harper, all my anger comes pouring out at him.

I charge, words coming out my mouth, but I can't hear what I'm saying. I charge him like I'm gonna take him out for letting Boo go. For not coming after me and Mama when I was a baby. For thinking I'm just some gangbanging fool. For just giving up on all these horses and the stables and the Cowboy Way.

The next thing I know, I'm hitting him. He sinks to his knees like he got no strength left, but I don't stop. I know everyone looking at me, but I can't keep it in no more. I don't care what nobody thinks of me. I just gotta hit somebody or I'm gonna bust.

Somehow, he gets his arms around me, and I try to fight him off, but he don't let go. He holds on like I'm a storm in his arms, and I give it all I got till he slowly smothers that anger and all the fight goes out of me too.

I'm breathing hard, my heart racing. He holds me close, and I let him. Tears is coming down my face, but it don't matter now. I don't care if everybody sees me crying. I got nothing left.

I can feel the other guys around us, talking all quiet, but I can't make it out. Finally, I hear Bob whisper in his ear, "Harper, what are we gonna do?"

Harper takes a deep breath and says quietly, "I don't know."

He looks around at everyone standing there, like they all waiting for his command. "I got to think," he says, and he gets up and walks off toward the Ritz-Carlton.

The other guys look at each other and scowl. The suit said they had twenty-four hours to move their horses out, but no one seem to know where to take 'em. Tex says all the stables that woulda taken them is full up or been closed up by the City already. Everything else is too expensive or over in Jersey.

Somebody jokes that they could take all the horses up the Appalachian Trail and hide 'em. Another guy says maybe the Federation of Black Cowboys in Brooklyn will take 'em. I look at him and imagine a cavalry of black cowboys coming to save the day. He shrugs. "We aren't the only black cowboys out there, you know."

Most of 'em look like they got their hearts ripped out of their chests. Some of the kids is off crying or standing around looking like somebody ran over their dog. They look totally lost. Some of the guys is angry, kicking at a trash can or yelling at each other. But nobody is talking about how they gonna save the horses and the stables. They all thinking about themselves.

Me, I just look where Boo was standing and make a promise: *I will get you back, Boo. No matter what, I will get you back.*

I look around for Harper and find him in the Ritz, glaring up at that big ol' hole in the roof. The blue tarp is hanging down inside, and he grabs it, trying to pull it down. The more it gets stuck, the more he starts pulling on that thing like if it's the last thing he do, he gonna pull it down. I can see the anger in him building up, and for a second, I think he gonna pull the roof down on top of him.

Then I hear some music—sounds like that Coltrane guy. Harper ignores it, but it keeps going until he reaches in his pocket and pulls out his cell phone. He flips it open, and the music stops. He stares at the caller ID and sees me almost at the same time.

He don't talk to the phone, just holds it out for me. "It's for you."

There's only one person I can think of who would call me.

I grab the phone and I listen. I can hear someone breathing on the other end. "Mama?" I ask.

I hear her exhale. "Baby," she says, barely a whisper.

I stand there for a long time, just listening to her breathe. Harper looks at me, then leaves. Finally, Mama asks, "How you doing, Cole?"

It's what she used to say to me when I woke up in the morning and wandered into the kitchen. *How you doing, Cole?*

I stare at the hole in the roof, and it feels like the hole in my stomach. Everything that's happened since she left me here is running through my head. I don't know how to answer that question.

"Baby?" she asks.

I got nothing to say.

She starts talking. "I been thinking . . . maybe—"

"Maybe what?"

She sighs. "Maybe I made a mistake."

Maybe.

I'm looking out the barn door, seeing all the guys arguing. Harper's just staring off into space like he lost. A couple days ago, I woulda just said come get me. Now, I don't know. I don't know what I'm thinking, but with everything going on here, I don't feel like talking to her right now.

"Baby—" she says as I close the phone.

I stand there looking at the crushed stall where Boo was. It might be easier to go back to Mama instead of dealing with all a this. But I start getting this weird feeling in my gut. The only thing I can think of is the promise I made to Boo. I know I gotta go find him. I got to get him back. I see the guys giving up, but that don't seem like the Cowboy Way, not like Harp told it. What happened to never giving up, to having everyone's back, and treating your horse like your best friend? What happened to banding together like cowboys and standing up to the Man?

I head back out into the open. Some of the guys is already packing up, getting their horses ready to leave. Others is on their cell phones, trying to make arrangements. Harper's still standing there, looking around like it's already over.

"Harper."

He ignores me.

"Harper," I say again.

Without looking at me, he says, "You going home to Mama."

Maybe I didn't hear him right. "We gotta do something," I say.

He looks at me, his eyes red and tired out. "That wasn't a question. You got to go back. You got your schooling to attend to."

I'm tired of feeling like I been kicked in the face. "I ain't going back."

I see a little surprise in his eyes, but it goes away. "I can't take care of you, Cole. Not with all this going down. It's too much."

I look over at Tex, who's sittin' on a old worn-out couch, smoking a cigarette. He the only one who's calm.

"You ain't taking care of me no-how. So what

difference do it make?" I say. I can tell he don't like that I said that. "I can help," I add.

"No, you can't," he says. "This is serious."

I stand my ground. "You just gonna let 'em take this away too? Seem like that's all you do when things get tough—walk away."

He stares into the dirt. "You don't understand how things work in the real world. This ain't some cowboy fantasy. Sometimes you can't do nothing except keep moving on." Then he turns and starts to walk away.

"What kinda man is you?" I say, ready for a fight.

He stops. "What'd you say?"

I don't back down. "I said, what kinda man—"

That does it. He wheels around, his eyes wide, and for a second, I think he gonna kill me. "What kind of man am I?" he yells.

Harper grabs me by the shirt. "I'm the kind of man who took care of this whole neighborhood! I'm the man who kept this tradition alive! I'm the man who saved these horses from becoming dog food!" he spits. "I'm the man—" He towers over me, out of breath, out of words, like he gonna crush me. Suddenly, I don't wanna hear no more. I see Tex rushing over, and when Harper looks up at him, I bolt.

I run out of the stables and down the street. I run and I run till I can't breathe no more, till I can't

hear the yelling or nothing. I'll go rescue Boo myself.
The hell with Harper. The hell with all of 'em. They
want to give up, then fine. I'll rescue Boo myself and
then . . .

And then what? I think of them old stories Tex
told us, about cowboy justice and the Chisholm Trail.
What would a real cowboy do? Shoot 'em up? Run the
bad guys outta town? Maybe.

But right now, all them ideas seem a million miles
away.

TWENTY-SIX

I run until I hit the park. I scramble into the wild and get lost in the trees. I have this vision of me and Boo off in the country, running from the law, living off the land and having fires at night. Maybe I could take all the horses and we could go up to Brooklyn like Jamaica Bob said. Maybe there's a whole world of black cowboys up there. I ain't never been to Brooklyn, but maybe they have lots of land and could take us all in. I could work in their stables and maybe one day start racing Boo for real and earn my keep that way.

"Yo, Cole!"

I hear my name and realize I'm standing at the edge of the trees facing a bunch of guys playin' on a basketball court. Someone yells my name again, and I see my cousin Smush standing next to one of the baskets with a ball in his hand. Snapper's behind him, trying to take the ball away, but Smush is too quick. Finally, he rolls his eyes and tosses the ball to the others, and the game continues without him.

He shrugs. "What you doing out here, cuz?"

It takes me a second to refocus. He walks up to me.

"What's a matter, horse kick you in the head?"

"Ain't you heard?" I say.

He gives me a look that says he didn't. I tell him the whole story of the raid and them stealing the horses and how they gonna bulldoze the stables. His face gets gloomier and gloomier.

"I saw them cops whizzing by, but I just thought it was some drug bust or something. That's why I came out here."

He watches the game, but his mind is somewhere else. "That sucks for real. An' Harper's just gonna roll over? I can't believe that. Somebody's got to do something. I mean, I don't care for them horses so much, but they part of the neighborhood, you know?

143

Can't let the City get away with that. We need to go and kick some serious butt."

Finally, someone who wants to do something! "I got a plan," I say, and I explain about getting the horses and settin' them free.

He looks real skeptical, but I think he likes the danger part of it. "I don't know, cuz. Don't sound like much of a plan. You even know where them horses are? What kind of security you got to deal with? How you gonna ride all them horses outta there, and where you gonna go with 'em?"

I haven't thought that far yet. Smush frowns like he can tell my plan ain't so planned out yet.

He shrugs. "Still, any chance to get back at the Man is one I'm up for. Lucky for you, I'm hooked up. Let me make some calls."

He whips out his cell phone and hits speed dial. He walks around, talking real fast as he explains the situation to whoever he talking to. Then there's a series of back-'n'-forths. He ends the call with "Get back to me." Then he snaps his fingers, and Snapper comes running.

Smush goes through the whole story again, and I can see Snapper getting madder and madder at the City, and I think I wouldn't wanna be on his bad side.

When Smush gets to the end, they both turn toward me and suddenly I realize, I got me a posse.

"Well, cuz, you got our attention. What you wanna do?"

I smile. It feels good to be looked up to for once. "I just wanna get Boo and them other horses out. Then we can see about keeping them dudes from bulldozing the stables. We just gotta find out where they took 'em—"

Smush's phone rings, and he talks for a few seconds, then snaps it shut. "My man on the inside heard the horses was took to a stable here in the park. Only problem is, it's where the police horses are too."

Snapper scowls, but police don't bother me.

"Let's do it," I say.

TWENTY-SEVEN

We head away from the court, passing over the expressway. Smush tells me they built that thing so white folks could drive right over the neighborhood without stopping. It's real loud up there, but when we hit the other side of the park, it's like we in real nature. The sounds of the cars get farther and farther away. Smush seem to know his way around, so I don't ask no questions.

We head deep into the woods, moving along a creek. I just keep thinking about Boo and how scared he must be. I mean, he spooked enough as is, but after all this, he must be a head case for sure.

After seein' nothin' but trees for half an hour, we come to the edge of a clearing. I hear some hootin' and hollerin', and I see some white boys jumping off what looks like a cliff!

"That's the Devil's Pool," said Smush. "Only them crazy white kids go there."

We round the bend, and I can see the kids was diving into a deep pool of water way down off the cliff. It feels like we in the middle of the jungle out there with wild boys living off the land.

We pass through some more woods, and then Smush says, "Slow up." We come to the back of a old stone building, and I can smell it from here: horses.

We walk around until we see a outdoor corral and stables. And sure enough, there're a coupla cops in cowboy hats brushing down their rides.

I can't believe it. "You really got sheriffs here! Dag, you don't see that in Detroit."

Smush don't look impressed. "They can be on a horse or in a squad car; they still police."

I look around, and on the far end of the corral I

hear Boo. He makes a noise, and suddenly I see him in a open stall and he looking right at me, even though we way across the way. That Boo must have bionic vision or something.

"Boo!" I say out loud, but Smush hushes me and pulls me back behind a tree. The cop don't see me, so we sneak around to the other side and come up on the fence of Boo's stall. Boo sees us right away and sticks his nose in between the opening.

"Good ol' Boo. You okay, boy?" I stick my hand in through the fence and pet him. He neighs, which I take for a yes, then snorts all over my arm.

Smush makes a face. "Man, I don't know why you wanna get this old horse out. You better off gettin' a bike. You don't gotta feed it or clean up after it. Just gotta ride it."

I ignore him. "We gonna get him out, okay? If you afraid of them cops, you can go on home. I'll do it by myself."

Snapper shakes his head. "Oh, now you the Terminator, just gonna walk in and walk right out with all them horses."

Smush sucks on his teeth. "I ain't gonna ditch you, cuz. I'm just saying it ain't the smartest plan in the world."

"I'm not leaving him in jail."

That makes Smush laugh. "Cuz, I wish jail was like this, then I wouldn'ta minded spending the summer there. So what do you wanna do, genius?"

I look around. There's one gate into the main corral area with the outdoor stalls. The stalls don't seem to have any locks or nothing. Seem pretty simple to me. "We wait until it gets dark, then we go in."

Smush pulls me back down. "Okay. Saying we get the horses, then what?"

I look at him. "Then we ride."

"Ride where?"

I tell him what the guys said about the Federation of Black Cowboys.

"Brooklyn? Now I know you crazy. That's like two hours away by car! What, you just gonna ride all them horses on the expressway? Cuz, you lost your head."

"What's the difference between Harp and them riding in the streets and this?" I ask.

"About a hundred miles," he says.

I shake him off. "Look, let's just get 'em outta here, then we'll figure it out. Harper says this park is so big you can get lost in it. So we'll get lost, hide out, and figure our next move. We can camp in these woods here, like we on the run."

"Not *like*. We *will* be on the run." He stares at the cop through the fence. "I don't know, cuz. I'm already on probation. If I get caught . . ."

I give him a little push. "Like I said, if you can't man up—"

He pulls his fist back like he gonna pop me, then smiles when he sees I'm playin' him.

"You lucky you my cuz, or you'd be eatin' dirt."

TWENTY-EIGHT

We sit back in the shadows and wait. Smush is playing with his phone, texting and looking at videos.

Snapper's looking at me, probly wondering about what I got him into. "You should really talk to Harp about this. He won't want you breaking the law," he says.

I shake my head. "Look, Harp has to do what he has to do. He already got Lightning living in his house and that's all he gotta worry about. They gonna sell off ol' Boo for dog food—I know it."

Snapper makes a face. "Dogs eat horse? Man, that's messed up."

Smush looks up from his phone. "Wait a sec. How come the City rescues these horses only to destroy 'em? That don't make no sense."

I shrug. "All I know is, these ain't prize horses or nothing. They has-beens. You think the police wants seconds from people like us?"

Smush nods. "You got a point." He glances down at his phone screen and gets a weird look on his face. He brings it up to his face and watches more closely. "Oh, damn. Check it out. We on the news!"

He holds up his phone and shows me a video. I see the inspection dudes going through the Ritz-Carlton, examining horses, talking about the bad conditions they lived in and how the stables was illegal and all. They show everything—the hole in the roof, all the mud and muck, that big pile of crap, but worse of all, the dead horse.

Seeing it this way, it looks bad. Suddenly, I can see how someone watching this would think the cops is the good guys and *we* the bad guys. Like everyone who live around here must be too poor or too stupid to take care of their pets. They'll wonder what we thinkin' keepin' horses in the middle of a war zone in the worst neighborhood in Philly. That's how it looks to me, and I know better!

Smush stares at the video. "You can't believe nothing you see on the news. No one has the right to do what they doing to Uncle Harp and these horses.

They just looking to stir things up to make a story."

When he says that, suddenly I know Jamaica Bob was right—the City wants that land and will do *anything* to get it. "They musta planned to raid the stable after that storm, knowin' it'd make us look bad," I say. "And maybe they let that crap pile up just for something like this, so they could get it on video."

Smush nods. "Makes sense now. I mean, how else would the news even get this video, unless the City gave it to them?"

"Dang, that's like a conspiracy!"

"Yeah, a conspiracy. That's what it is," says Smush, shaking his head. "Man, we in it now!"

Snapper interrupts. "Look, they on the move," he says, pointing at a few guys taking the horses into the stone building on the far side of the corral.

I see one of 'em leading Boo inside. "Dag, now what we gonna do? We got to break in there too!"

Smush tells me to be quiet. "We'll figure it out," he says, like he has no idea. "Just sit tight."

When the sun goes down, the park feels different. It's dark an' empty, the trees is kinda spooky. I ain't never been in a forest at night, but with us being quiet, all kind of animals and who knows what seem to come alive around us. It's like the forest is a living, breathing thing. All them pretty trees from before look kinda crazy now, like monsters.

We watch them guys who was working with the horses drive off one by one. After they gone, it feels pretty quiet. Just a light on in one of the upstairs windows in the stone building.

"Should we go in now?" Snapper asks.

Smush is listening. "We should wait a little longer to make sure."

But I can't wait. I keep thinking about Boo becoming dog food. "Nah, they all left." I start climbing the fence. "We got to go in now."

Smush and Snapper look at each other and shrug. They follow.

We get into the main corral and then run to the shadows of the stone building. The whole place seem empty.

"We better make sure that main gate opens. Otherwise we'll just be trapped in this yard once we get the horses out the building," Smush says.

Snapper takes out a pair of bolt cutters. "I'm on it." He sees me staring. "What? You never know when you'll need these bad boys." He runs over and starts fiddling with the gate.

We sneak to the edge of the building and try a old wood door. It opens. Inside, there's a long line of stalls on both sides, and I can hear horses moving about. I don't see no guards or no cameras looking over the room. So we sneak in like a coupla ninjas, peekin' in each stall for any of Harper's horses. The horses watch us closely, but they don't do nothing. Some is even sleeping standing up.

I go down the whole row and don't see nobody I know, 'specially not Boo. "Maybe they already took 'em away when we wasn't looking!" I say, starting to panic.

Then I hear Boo give a little horse neigh. I'm no expert, but I come to know Boo's sounds. I run over to another wood door on the far end of the room and slide it open. It's dark inside, but there, behind a chain-link fence, is Boo, his eyes all big and watery. It ain't nice at all, not like the other horses have. Boo's standing there, his face pressed against the fence, looking all sad. The other eight horses is in there too.

"We gonna get you guys outta here, Boo," I whisper to him.

There's a big ol' padlock on the fence, but when Snapper takes a look, he has that thing off in two seconds flat. I'm about to open it when Smush stops me.

"Now, you sure about this? So far, we ain't done nothing illegal, but you take them horses, and that's stealing."

I already thought this through. "It ain't stealing if it's yours. They stole 'em first. I'm just taking 'em back. It's called cowboy justice."

Smush shakes his head. "Okay, then, cowboy. Lead the way."

TWENTY-NINE

I push open the gate and walk up to Boo. I remember the first time I saw him and how big he seemed and how scared I was that he'd step on me. Now it feels okay, like we watching out for each other. I pet his neck, and he brushes his head against my shoulder.

"My man, Boo . . ."

Suddenly, we hear a noise coming from upstairs. Definitely the sound of footsteps.

Smush peeks in the door. "Cuz, we ain't got time for no reunions. We got to get 'em outta here."

The horses don't got no saddles, but we don't got the time to saddle 'em up, anyway. "Help me up on Boo," I say.

Smush looks doubtful. "You ever rode bareback before?"

I think of the last time Boo dumped me without a saddle. "We don't got no choice, do we?"

I grab Boo's mane as gently as I can, and Smush gives me a lift. When I get up there, it feels all weird, nothing to hold on to but his hair.

"You don't mind, do ya, Boo?" I ask.

He glances back at me, like, *What you doing back there?* But he seem okay with it. "Okay, now you guys get on them horses. The other six will just have to follow us on their own."

Smush hops up pretty easy, but Snapper balks. "I ain't getting up there. You crazy?"

There's some more scuffling going on upstairs. Smush looks tense. "Snap, you best mount up. I know you ain't afraid of no horse."

Snapper scowls. He tries to get up on the horse, but it keeps moving around in circles. "You trying to wake the neighbors?" I say. "You got to act confident, like you know what you doing." *Where'd I hear that before?*

Snapper glares at me like he gonna knock me off. "I ain't afraid," he says, all steely. He stares down his horse. "You move again, and I'll knock *you* out."

I think the horse believes him, 'cause he don't move again. Snapper gets up, though it ain't pretty. He seem worried for a second until he sees me looking at him.

"What? I can ride. I just don't like to."

The horses is getting antsy. I whisper in Boo's ear. "Okay, Boo, you gotta lead the way. The other horses will follow you."

He nods his head. Smush acts surprised.

"Maybe he as crazy as you," Smush says.

I click my tongue and try to steer him out the room. Boo moves slowly into the stall area but stops halfway through. I can hear more shuffling upstairs.

"Come on, Boo. We ain't got all day—"

Someone drops something heavy upstairs, and suddenly Boo takes off. Not like racing, but a real fast walk, like you do when you know you gonna get caught. Fast enough that I almost fall off. I'm grabbing all around for something to hang on to, but there ain't nothing. I squeeze my legs and pull back on his mane a little. He neighs and eases up by the front door.

"Quiet, Boo," I hiss. "Don't get all spooked on me."

Someone nudges Boo from behind. Smush's horse. I turn around, and after Smush, only Snapper and his horse is there. The others didn't follow! Smush can see what I'm thinking.

"They ain't dogs—they horses. What'd you expect?"

Suddenly, someone in front of us shouts, "Hey! What're you doing?"

He don't sound happy. I whip back around and see some guy carrying a trash can blocking our way. Before I can think of some crazy excuse, Boo takes off right toward the guy! This time, I fall sideways and I fight to hold on, almost kicking that dude in the face as we fly by.

The front gate to freedom that Snapper broke open earlier is barely open now, so Boo turns left and runs along the corral fence instead of going through the gate. I can't see what's going on behind me, but Boo stops for a second, long enough for me to try and right myself and see that janitor dude coming our way.

He trying to get in Boo's way, but Boo ain't backing off. Behind him, I can see Smush and Snapper busting a move for the front gate. Smush jumps off his horse and opens it all the way and waves me over.

"Stop messing around! We gotta go!" he yells.

I roll my eyes, then kick Boo in the side, which he don't like too much. He steps toward the dude, who's clearly not a horse guy. He holds his trash can in front of him like a shield, but Boo just brushes him aside and follows Smush out the front gate.

As we head out into the darkness, I can see the guy running back inside the stone building. Probly gonna call the cops. But I don't care, 'cause I kept my promise—I freed Boo.

THIRTY

Smush leads the way through the forest, holding a little flashlight in his mouth 'cause he gotta hold on to his horse. Snapper follows but looks like he never rode before, which is probly what I look like too. I think about them other horses we left behind and maybe how we shoulda gone back for 'em. But what's done is done, and I'm just glad we got Boo. I wrap my arms around Boo's neck and bounce like crazy as he trots along. He seem happy to be out in the open again.

When we get deep into the trees, Smush eases up. "We got to hang low. Cops'll be patrolling for some black horse thieves, so it ain't like they won't know it's us. I know a place where we can hide out in the park till dawn. Then maybe it'll be quiet enough to head out."

He whips out his phone and says to someone, "Meet us at the Devil's Pool. And bring food and sleeping bags. Yeah, we going camping! Just do it!"

The horses move along slowly, 'cause it's dark, and riding without a saddle is near impossible. I start thinkin' about what Tex said 'bout the Old West, but I don't suppose this is what the Chisholm Trail was like. It's pitch-black out, and all kinda weird noises is going on in that darkness. I don't know how Smush finds his way. I can't tell which way we headin'—it all feels the same to me.

When we finally get close to the spot, we have to go super slow 'cause the trail's all rocky. Smush keeps pointing his light into the pit where the pool is. It's like it drops into the center of the Earth.

We stop in a little clearing.

"Okay, this is good a place as any," Smush says, hopping off.

"What about the horses?" I ask. "We can't just leave 'em be. They might run off into that pit."

Smush smiles, then holds up a rope he has around his shoulder. "Snagged it on the way out. We can tie 'em up."

I watch him pull out a knife and start cutting off long pieces. I start thinking about what kinda trouble I got us into. I don't even want to think about what Harp might do to me. So I try to think about something else instead. Like food. "I'm hungry."

Smush pats me on the back. "Food's coming. Don't expect nothing fancy."

I look over and see the horses munching on some grass and weeds. "Looks like they ain't gonna wait for us."

We sit in the dark. The blackness is starting to weigh down on us, but Smush tries to lighten the mood. "So, I guess you a outlaw now. We should give you a nickname, like the Kid or something."

Snapper laughs. "How 'bout the Motown Mutt?"

Smush shakes his head. "Nah, we'll just call him Motor City from now on."

I don't like that neither. "I don't think so."

Smush snaps his fingers. "I got it. We'll call you the Train, like Coltrane, get it?"

Train. Yeah, that seem about right. Like everybody gonna hop on board and we gonna go places!

"That's okay," I say, playing it down.

Smush grins. "Train it is, then. But you better call your daddy so he don't think the Train's derailed."

He pops open his phone and hits speed dial, then hands it to me.

"What'll I say?"

"Tell him you having a sleepover with your friends," cracked Snapper.

I listen to the rings. Harper finally picks up, but he don't sound too happy.

"Smush, you know where my boy's at?"

I don't say nothing.

"Smush?"

"It's me. Cole."

There is a long silence on the other end.

"Where are you?" he finally says.

I don't know what to tell him, so I just start talking.

"I got Boo. And a couple others. The rest stayed—"

He don't let me finish. "What do you mean, you got Boo? Where the hell are you?"

"We hiding in the park."

"Fairmount Park? And who's 'we'? You and Smush?"

"And Snapper."

There's a long pause, and I can almost feel the

heat from Harp's anger coming through the phone. "So, let me get this straight. You and those corner boys gone and stole the horses from some government facility—"

"We were saving 'em! Somebody had to!"

"Yeah? Is that what you're gonna tell the judge when he sends you off to juvie?"

"Well, at least I did something—"

"Yeah, you became another statistic—that's what you did. Just like Smush, another black stereotype of a hoodlum—"

"It's not like that! Smush was doing what I told him to. He was trying to help!"

"Help? How is that going to help? For years, we been working with kids to get them off the streets. But all that's out the window now, because apparently, we're just training hoods!"

"But—"

"Once the City gets wind of this, it'll be over! You hear me!? What kind of son are you?"

I can't listen no more. "I ain't your son and you ain't my daddy, so you can go to hell!" I say, and hang up. I'm breathing hard, staring into the darkness.

Finally Smush speaks up. "I guess he wasn't too happy about what we done."

Ya think? I don't even bother answering him.

Smush and Snapper sit down on a rock and talk in whispers. I don't care what they saying.

"Can't we light a fire or something?" I ask.

Smush says no. It'll cause too much attention. So we sit in the dark and wait.

THIRTY-ONE

After a long time passes, maybe hours, the horses start to get nervous. Then I see some light flickering through the trees.

"Looks like we got company," says Snapper, and he scrambles up the rocks.

After a minute, he come rushing back. "Must be the mounted police. We gotta go."

Smush and me scramble up the rock for a look. There's four of 'em on horses with flashlights.

"Maybe if we keep quiet, they won't come up this way," I whisper.

Then I hear, "Coltrane!"

It's Harper.

He in the lead, and then I recognize Jamaica Bob and Tex behind him.

"How'd they find us?" I ask.

Smush sees the fourth guy. One of his crew. "Sold out by one of my own," he says. "This ain't gonna be pretty."

Harper's light swings up and finds us. He don't say nothing.

"Busted," says Smush.

They come around the bend and stop. Harper's light shines on us, then checks out the horses. Nobody says nothing. Finally, Tex climbs down.

"Heard you needed supplies," he says, undoing a coupla bags on his horse. "Got some food, drinks, blankets."

Harper slowly gets off his horse and passes Smush, who tries to explain. "Uncle Harp, it wasn't his fault—"

Harp just holds up his hand, saying, "I'll talk with you later."

Then he comes up to me, grabs my arm. "Come with me."

I don't really have a choice, do I?

We walk over to the edge of the pit. I look down into the darkness, thinking he gonna throw me in. He stands there, breathing slowly, not saying nothing. Finally, I can't take it no more.

"It was all my idea. I'm the one who talked Smush into helping. So if you gonna do it, do it now."

He looks confused, then sees me looking into the pit.

"I'm not gonna throw you in, Coltrane, even though I should."

He sits down on the edge, tosses a rock down into the pit. I hear a splash not too far down.

He sighs. "I been trying to figure out why this life is so hard," he says. "Why they out to get us? Is it because we're cowboys? Or is it just because we're black?"

I know what he's saying. I feel like we the Pistons from way back when. They was always the underdogs, always counted out. No one liked 'em because they didn't play by the rules. But they kept fighting, no matter what, until they became champs. "Maybe it's 'cause they don't like anyone that's different. Anyone they can't understand or control is bad news to them."

He looks at me and nods.

I sit down next to him. "You mad at me for getting them horses out?"

"Yeah, but not for the reason you think," he says. "My whole life has been about them horses. It's why your mama left, 'cause I was too stubborn to change or give 'em up. I know I cared more about them than her at the time." He looks back at the horses, chewing on grass. "Then you came along, and I guess it seemed like too much. I couldn't handle it. I kind of disappeared for a while. Took my horse up onto the Appalachian Trail and just headed north. By the time I got my head straight and made it back home, you and her was gone."

We sit there, listening to the wind blowing through the trees. Harper is silent for a long time.

"You coming back here made me realize how much I hate losing something that I care about." He clears his throat. "Even if things were finished between me and your mama, I shoulda been there for you." He puts his hand on my knee. "I know you ain't no gangbanging fool. And I know you didn't drive your mama away. I'm sorry I said that before."

I don't know what to say to that, but it feels good to hear.

"I need to do better. I *will* do better," he says. "Starting with us figuring out how to get out of this mess. But we'll do it together—you and me, okay?"

Together. Suddenly, my posse just got bigger.

He elbows me in the side, all playful. "At least you was trying to get those horses back, even if it was a boneheaded idea." He stands up and stares into the pit. And then he asks, "So what other ideas you got in that head of yours?"

I think of how they done things in the Old West. Poor folks fighting off land barons and all a that stuff.

"If we let them bulldoze the Ritz, there might not be no more cowboys left in North Philly after that," I say. "It'll give 'em an excuse to say the last stables in the 'hood is just as bad, and they'll close them down too."

"So where does that leave us?" he asks, like he can't think no more.

From the movies I seen, I know one thing: Clint Eastwood wouldn'ta given up in a land war. "We gotta find a way to get some attention, so people can hear *our* side of the story, not just what the news been showing. City thinks they can shut us down and nobody'll care. But if we can get the *people* of Philly on our side . . ."

And suddenly, I can see it. A whole lot of people standing in the way of those bulldozers, the cowboys out in front, representin'. "What if we did some kind of blockade thing, with horses and everything? You know, show 'em what we stand for?"

He shrugs. "Might get us arrested."

I nod. "Yeah, but don't you think that would get us on TV?"

He smiles and then starts to laugh. "Looks like you a cowboy after all."

THIRTY-TWO

We head back to the others. Tex and Jamaica Bob have put ropes and blankets on the horses to make it easier to ride.

"So, what's the verdict?" asks Tex.

Harper puts his hand on my shoulder. "Boy says we should fight back. Says we got to stand up for what we believe in. And I tend to agree with him. Moving our horses somewhere else is what they want, but fighting to keep these stables open, that's the right thing to do. It's the cowboy thing to do."

Tex lets out a cheer. "Hot damn! I'm ready to fight!"

Smush holds him back. "Take it easy, old man. You gonna give yourself a heart attack!"

I explain my idea to them, how we gonna get every last horseman from any stables left in North Philly to stand in front of them bulldozers. Smush looks uneasy about maybe getting arrested, but then he says, "You can't stop a moving train!"

He and Jamaica Bob and Harper all get on their cell phones and start making calls. They up for hours, eating, making calls, getting organized. I try to grab a

few Z's. By the time they finish, the sky is starting to get light again.

Harper stands. "We should go, boys. We got to be in place by eight a.m., when the City shows up."

Bob and Tex offer to ride the horses with no saddles. Smush and Snapper get on horses with saddles, but nobody's gonna ride Boo but me. Harp understands.

We head out just as the sun's coming up over the park. We higher up, so it seem like you can see forever, trees and grass, and behind that the city loomin' up like a giant, waiting for us.

• • •

The streets is quiet. It feels like the world is still asleep, but as we get closer, I start hearing a noise. It sounds like something big and alive and grows louder and louder until suddenly I recognize what it sounds like—a big ol' crowd of people.

We round the corner to Chester Avenue, and I see something I never seen before. There must be seventy or eighty cowboys on horses milling about. Old heads and a bunch of young kids too. Even some white folks is there.

Harper sees my eyes go wide and winks at me. "*That* would be the cavalry."

Tex laughs. "Can you imagine the look on the City fellas' faces when they see this?" He slaps his leg. "If they expect us to just roll over, they got another thing coming!"

The others all spot us and start whistling and making cowboy hoots and hollers, slapping us on the back. Even Carmelo and Big Dee is there, treating us like kings, passing us our saddles and stuff.

Big Dee says, "Brothers, this is one showdown we ain't missing!"

Harper moves to the middle of everyone, but there's so many people, you can't really see him no more. Then suddenly, he standing above everyone, and I realize he standing up on Lightning's back!

He holds up his hands till everyone hushes. "You all know me as someone who don't back down from a fight." There's a lot of nodding and *Say it, brother!* going around. "But I was taken off guard this week and forgot what we're all about."

He searches for me until our eyes connect. "We may look like we're in the ghetto. But we're all working people, doing what we can to survive. We got our ways, and we got our traditions. Here on Chester Avenue, that means horses."

The guys are saying, *That's right,* petting their rides. "Now, most people on the outside may not understand our ways. They see these neighborhoods and think it's no place for animals. They think it's okay for *us* to live here, but poor folks can't have horses! They're used to horse owners with money, living the country life. But horses is like people: some come from money; some come from nothing. For these horses, the only thing between them and a can of dog food was us. They're the unwanted, just like us."

"Speak for yourself," says Big Dee. "I'm a stud!"

Harper smiles but keeps going. "The City acts

like they care about the animals, but they don't. They just after the land. And they'll do anything to get it. Including dividing us by making us look like we the bad guys."

I see more neighborhood people on foot gathering around us. Harper's eyes is shining bright now. "These kind folks out here know better. Our neighbors have put up with us through the years because they understood the value of what we're doing. Not that it's always been perfect—far from it. But we trying. We pour our hearts and souls into this way of life." He sighs, probly thinkin' about everything he put into the cause. "Now, I've been called many things in my life: an urban rider, a horseman, a pain in the butt." That gets some laughs. "But deep down, even if we don't all look like Tex here, we cowboys. We are *cowboys!*"

A cheer goes up from everyone, and while they making noise, Harp yells, "And cowboys stick together and defend their turf!"

Everybody stomping and clapping, and the kids is blowin' whistles and making a lotta noise. It's like the ground is shaking underneath us. Then I realize the ground *is* shaking underneath us!

Everyone hushes up, and we hear a rumbling sound coming from around the corner. Harper sits back down on the horse and makes his way to the front, next to me. We watch and wait.

"You scared, son?" he whispers.

I can't answer him 'cause my jaw seem like it's locked tight.

"Me too," he says. "But whatever happens, we do it together, okay?"

I nod.

THIRTY-THREE

A bulldozer comes around the corner, followed by a coupla big dump trucks and a few black cars. You can see the look of disbelief on the drivers' faces when they see us. Maybe we got the same look on ours. They all shaking their heads, like, *This is not what we needed.*

We block the entrance to the stables, and the bulldozer stops about twenty feet in front of us. The driver sits there, smoking his cigarette. I can see him thinking if he should just plow on through, but he don't make a move.

Finally, I see the fat dude in the suit from before come running up, looking all mad.

"What do you think you're doing?"

Harper don't bat an eye. "Protecting our neighborhood."

I pipe in, "We cowboys!"

The suit looks at us like we crazy.

Harper stares him down good. "We decided you can't destroy our way of life. Y'all never cared about this neighborhood, but these people here made something good for the community—from nothing but a bunch of empty, neglected lots. And we want it to stay that way."

The suit grinds his teeth. I can see him counting the crowd, trying to figure his next move. "So, what are your intentions?" he says.

Harper nods to me. "Tell him, Train." I look at him, and he winks. He musta heard my nickname from Smush.

I clear my throat. "We gonna stand here however long it takes for you to back down," I say, and I mean it. "We ain't going nowhere."

Harper smiles. "My son."

The guy's eyes look like they gonna bust outta his head. He reaches into his pocket and whips out a piece of paper. "I have an order from the City of Philadelphia, authorizing us to tear down this illegal stable!"

Tex makes his way up to the front. "It's our right to be here. This is our home. So we ain't leaving and that's that. The people have spoken, so you and that piece of paper best be on your way, ya hear?"

All the riders start cheering and whistling. The horses stomp their hoofs like they ready to stampede. I can see the suit is losin' his nerve. He starts backing up.

"I can have all of you arrested, you know!"

"Maybe," Smush jumps in. "But we still won't leave."

The suit turns and storms back to his car. I can see him talking on his cell phone. Some of our guys get out their phones too, videotaping everything and talking about posting it online to get some attention.

We at a standstill for a good hour. The waiting starts to get boring, but nobody moves. Then a coupla cop cars show up.

The guy in the suit starts getting all excited again, pointing at us and stuff. The cops look like they have better things to do than mess with us. After a minute, one of the cops comes up to us.

It's Harper's friend Leroy.

Harper shakes his head. "So this is what the City of Brotherly Love has come to. . . . They send *you* to come in and divide us?"

Leroy don't look happy. "I'm here because I want to keep this from getting out of hand. Now, I don't suppose you fellas got a permit to protest?"

We all look at each other, but Harper just shakes his head and says, "The real question you should be asking is, are you gonna be with us or with them?"

Leroy sighs and looks at everyone. "Harp, you know I support all of you. But this is my job. I will do whatever I can to fix this situation, but I can't break the law, can I?"

Harper sucks on his teeth, thinking. "It's our right to protect our land, or am I missing something?"

Leroy grumbles. "Look, Harp. It's outta my hands. This ain't the Wild West, okay? This is North Philly. And that there is city property according to the records. I'm sorry, but the City wants to reclaim its land."

Harper yells back. "After what? Neglecting it for a hundred years? After letting us rot down here all this time, suddenly *now* they take an interest? Because now they can make money on us? You know what's going down, man!"

"I know, Harp." Leroy kicks at the ground. "I know all too well. Been through it when they closed my stable down. I'm just asking you to work with me here, okay?"

Harper eases up. "Sorry." He takes out a piece of paper. "This here says that we got a right to unclaimed land after twenty-one years of habitation and taking care of it. We been using this property since 1951, and that means we have legal claim on it now. It's called squatters' rights."

Leroy glances at it. "This is from the Internet."

Harper takes the paper back. "It says we got the legal precedent! That means it's been done before."

Leroy sighs. "Look, that still don't mean you can block the street—"

"We're not moving!" someone shouts.

I turn and see Jamaica Bob staring at something past Leroy. "Look!" he says.

I see a white van coming down the street with a *Action News* sign on the side. Bob grins. "We gonna be on TV!"

Leroy sees the TV crew get out and start filming. "Great," he mutters, turning back to us. "Look, I'll hold off my guys as long as I can, but I can't promise anything. You guys do what you need to, but don't give them any excuses to—" He stops when the TV crew is in hearing range.

Harper whispers: "To what, arrest us? Now, there's an idea. That would look good on the news tonight.

I'm sure the City would love to see the cops on TV harassing honest folks and kids as they express their right to assemble and protect their livelihood."

Leroy grumbles. "You may be my friend, but deep down, you are one twisted—"

A TV newswoman interrupts him. "Are you going to arrest these cowboys, Officer?"

Leroy smiles for the camera but keeps his eyes on Harper. "Yeah, that one, for being ugly. No more comments."

THIRTY-FOUR

Leroy walks back to his car and gets on the radio. The TV woman sees me and holds out a microphone. "Young man, why are you here today?"

I gape at the microphone. Then I hear Smush say, "Tell her, Train! It's time people heard our side!"

I take a deep breath. "It's the Cowboy Way . . . to stand up for yourself when everything is against you."

"And who's against you? The City?" she asks.

"Yeah. See, these guys put everything they got into the stables, and they do it for free. They don't ask anyone for money, and they really helping the neighborhood way more than what the City does, which is nothin'."

Harp nods and jumps in. "Look, we make do with what we got, but we have enough to feed the horses and keep 'em happy. We've saved horses from the slaughterhouses, and more importantly, helped kids by giving them something else to do besides gangbangin', you know, teaching them to be responsible for another living being, instead of ending someone else's life."

Bob gets in on the action. "But the City don't care that this tradition has been going on for decades! Instead of celebrating something unique in this city, they just want us out of here so they can build a buncha new houses that we can't afford to live in!"

She nods and turns back to me. "So do you feel the City isn't giving you a fair shake?"

I think hard before answering. "To me, it feels like these City dudes waited till it stormed and the stables was full of mud and the place looked bad and run-down before they swooped in with their cameras. But there was nothing wrong with the horses they took. I mean, look at Boo! He look all right, don't he?"

When Boo hears his name, I swear he stares right into the camera like he a movie star or something. The reporter pets him on the neck and smiles. "Looks like Boo is ready for his close-up!"

They stop filming, but just as they about to move on to another shot, a big black police bus screeches to a halt behind the bulldozers. The suit leads a group of cops out, and suddenly it feels like things is gonna get ugly.

"Stand tall, fellas! Looks like they plan to haul us out of here!" yells Tex.

A lot of the guys stand up on their saddles, like Harper done. Even Smush does it. I know I'd fall off if I stood up, so I try to look as tall as I can instead.

Leroy comes back, shaking his head at the sight of the guys towering over him. "You're not making my life any easier, guys. On top of everything else, I have a report here that some horses were stolen from the Fairmount stables last night."

Boo shuffles, like he understood. I pat his neck. He getting nervous, like he thinks Leroy is gonna take him back.

"You can't steal what's yours!" someone in the back shouts. Snapper.

"A janitor said it was a bunch of teenagers." Leroy stares right at me. "You wouldn't know anything about that, would you, son?"

I look away, like I didn't hear him. I can feel the sweat rolling down my neck. His eyes is still on me, and I feel like I gotta say something or it'll look like the guys is a bunch of thieves. I start to open my mouth—

"It was me. I did it," Smush says.

I give him a sideways glance, like, *Whatchou doing?*

"I was there too. I did it."

I whip around and see Tex with his hand raised.

Then Jamaica Bob pipes up. "Me too. I was there."

Suddenly everyone, even the kids, is saying, *It was me. I did it,* until I say it too.

Leroy looks at the TV crew who's filming it all, then back at us. I think he knows it was me.

"You like that horse, son?" he asks.

I nod. "He's my horse. Sir."

He sighs, scratches his neck, then says loud enough for the suit and the cameras to hear, "Well, as it turns out, I made a call to the vet who checked out those horses that were taken from the stables yesterday. He said that, contrary to what was originally suspected, the horses were *not* malnourished and that they were actually in pretty good shape."

The guys get all quiet, then Leroy actually smiles a tiny bit. "So . . . all charges of animal endangerment have been dropped, and the City has agreed to return the rest of your horses."

A cheer goes up as the guys wave their hats. The suit throws a fit and starts yelling at the other cops, who just shrug.

"*But—*" Leroy holds up his hand.

"Here we go," says Tex.

"That still doesn't solve your two biggest problems: building-code violations and land rights. Now, I've made some phone calls, and in light of everything, you have been granted *one* week to upgrade your facilities to code. Do that, and they can't use it as an excuse to tear down the stables. As for who has the rights to that land, that'll be up to the courts to decide. That's the best I can do."

I look over at the stables and think, *One week?* Maybe one month or even a year. That place needs some serious work.

"We'll take what we can get," Harper says, shaking Leroy's hand. "Thanks, man."

Harper soaks in the scene. I can see him lookin' at the newspeople and all the crowds gathered around. Then he gets a look in his eyes. I can almost see the wheels in his head startin' to turn. He grins for the cameras.

"Philadelphia! Last year when they shut down the Bunker stables, the crime rate rose in that area because the teens had nothing to do but get in trouble. Support your local culture *and* help the kids by giving them something healthy to do with their time! Horses, not crime! Come lend a hand and help keep North Philly safe *and* special!"

The suit's not happy watching all this go down. "I'll be back in one week, and believe me, we'll have that bulldozer ready."

I give him the evil eye. "You do what you gotta do, mister. We'll be here."

Jamaica Bob shouts out, "Say it, brother Train!"

When I look around, I can see the crowd is twice as large now. I guess word got out around the neighborhood, and folks showed up. They come up to Harper, saying they'll do whatever they can to help. Some people is carpenters, some electricians, some handymen; some is just kids who don't know nothing. But a body is a body that can help out somehow.

When everyone leaves and things calm down, suddenly the situation don't look so rosy. There's a lot of work ahead. Harper gets all serious, then starts writing out a week's worth of work on a pad of paper, with a list just for me. It's a crazy-long list, but he says I should consider it community service for going behind his back and taking the horses.

I can't argue with that.

THIRTY-FIVE

That week, I work harder than my whole life put together. My entire body hurts. My arms. My legs. My back. But I keep going 'cause everybody else does too.

Harper shows me how to build stuff, how to hammer and saw and measure stuff right. I help them repair the roof, but this time, I stay on the ground. There's always ten things going on at once. But nobody complains. Even people who have nothing to do with riding show up carting spare wood, roofing stuff, equipment.

Leroy even shows up to help give that poor dead horse a proper burial. We all stop working when he hauls it away in a big oversize truck. I try not to think how it got here, with the accident an' all. That just makes me think of Mama, and then I feel bad for hanging up on her.

I do think about calling her back sometimes, but it's been way too crazy this week. Seems like we up at dawn and asleep as soon as we walk back in the house. Maybe when things quiet down some, I'll figure out what to say to her.

In between building and fixing stuff, the guys make me take care of the horses and show me a thing or two. Like how to brush 'em proper-like, how to put the saddle on, how to clean out their hoofs, stuff like that. Even that kid CJ and a few of his friends show up wanting to help. Everyone is so busy, I put them to work myself, doing some of the grooming and feeding, stuff I learned. They seem like they excited just to be doing it, and I said if they did a good job, they could start riding too. Harp saw me teaching them and put me in charge of finding them stuff to keep 'em busy. I like that.

A lot of the older kids and me go for rides with the guys around the neighborhood after a hard day's work.

Boo seem to trust me pretty good now. He even gallops a bit, and Harper shows me a few racing tricks, saying I'll be good to go at the Speedway soon if I keep it up.

Luckily, the rain stays away and the sun dries out everything pretty good. Soon, most things is looking better. Some gardening guy saw us on the news and said he'd help us get rid of that big ol' pile of crap by giving it to some urban-gardening projects all around the city. Said that stuff really makes vegetables grow great, which probly explains why I hate vegetables. It took him and us like a whole day to get the job done, but in the end, the lot looked pretty good. After that, we even heard a rumor that 'cause a the news, the City was gonna start picking this stuff up again. That would make my life a lot easier.

The Ritz-Carlton's looking more solid—not new but better, with a roof that looks like it'll hold up during the next storm. We also built some outside structures for the horses to stand under during a rain or to keep the sun off. Some of the neighbors even started talking about making a garden project of their own on one of the vacant lots. So things is looking up.

But money is tighter than ever and even after all that, the guys seem to have doubts that the stables will be around for long. A few say we'd won the battle, but the City will win the war sooner or later.

Some of the horses leave when guys find other stables outside the city. Harper don't stop 'em. He understands. He calls one of the reporters and says we need a lawyer to help represent ourselves in court so we can keep the land. There's a few leads, but not much.

When the week's up, Harper seem real nervous. We'd spent the day before the inspection really cleaning up the horses and making sure they looked healthy and nice. I even brushed Boo's teeth.

We hear the news guys ain't coming back to do a follow-up, and most the guys ain't surprised 'cause doing the right thing for the neighborhood ain't sexy or violent enough to make the news. But one of the kids who's helping out said he gonna video the whole inspection in case anything fishy goes down. The inspectors show up, but the dude in the suit ain't there. The inspectors go on a tour with Harper, who explains all the work we done and how the whole neighborhood pulled together.

After a hour, they leave, but it takes a whole other week before we hear back. Harper gets a letter at the stables one day. Everyone gathers around. He don't look too happy.

But then he grins and says we passed!

We about to all jump up and down, when he adds

that we've won only half the battle. "There's still the question of who has the rights to this land. We've taken a step in the right direction, and"—Harper looks at all of us proudly—"we're not going to give up now. We'll find a way to call this land our own. Even if we gotta buy it from the City to make it proper in everyone's eyes."

"Where we gonna get that kinda cash?" asks Tex.

Harp smiles and shrugs. "Haven't you seen the price of real estate around here? They should give us a rock-bottom price just to shut us up!"

Maybe. But still, it can't be that cheap. I start thinking of things we can do to raise money. I seen how good he is with the kids in the neighborhood. Maybe the schools would pay him to get the kids working with horses. Maybe Tex could show off some of his rodeo skills. You never know. . . .

THIRTY-SIX

One morning, I hear a bunch of noise downstairs and go down to find Harper taking Lightning out.

"Where y'all going?" I ask.

"Ol' Lightning here is moving back to the stables now that they're all fixed up. Besides, I'm tired of him making noise in the middle of the night."

I stare into his makeshift stall. "What you gonna do with that space?"

"Thought I'd have you clean it out."

I make a face. "Had enough of that kind of work. I need to rest for a month just to recover."

He shakes his head. "I was thinking it could maybe be your room, after we fix it up some, of course."

I give him a look. "You want me to *live* in there?"

He shrugs. "Hey, it was made for people first. Lightning was just a temporary renter, you know." He pats Lightning, like he thinking of something to say. "But if you want to, you know, stay here for real . . . this could be your room."

The room is dark and dirty, but I seen what we just done with the stable, so I can imagine it all fixed up nice with my own bed and stuff. It might be cool to have my own room. Even back home, I had to sleep on the couch.

"What happens if someone wants this place back?"

He steps outside, looks at the row houses around his, half boarded up. "No one will want it back 'cept us," he says sadly.

Then he looks at me and smiles. "Think about it. It'd be nice to have someone here who could clean up after himself."

I nod and watch him and Lightning go.

I wander into the kitchen to get some cereal, thinking about what my room could look like. I hear the door open and shut again, so I shout, "Don't tell me you changed your mind?"

"Yeah, Cole. I did."

I whip around and almost drop my bowl.

Mama.

We stand staring at each other for a long time. Half of me is real glad to see her. The other half still hates her for what she did. But there is still a part that knows I never woulda become a cowboy without her.

"Does Harper know you here?" I ask.

She shakes her head slowly.

"Why *are* you here?" I ask.

She struggles to say it. "I want you to come home, baby."

I open my mouth, but nothing comes out. Just when I was thinking maybe I could stay here, she shows up again. Just when I thought I might be okay without her, she wants me back.

I watch her as she stares at the broken wall, with Lightning's stall inside. She sighs. "I can't sleep at night. I don't like thinking of you living like this."

I put my bowl down. "It's okay. They taking care of me all right."

"They?" She looks surprised.

"Harp and the guys at the stables. I been learning to ride and all. I helped them build the barn up and stuff."

She moves toward me. "I miss you, Cole."

I step back. I don't feel like hugging her. She stops, searches for something to say. "I wasn't trying to punish you, Cole."

I know that. I look at the rings under her eyes and I know that. But why can I forgive Harp and not her? "We doing okay," I say, knowing the *we* gotta hurt.

But she takes it, 'cause she knows she has to. "I'm getting help now."

That throws me. "Help?" I say. "Why *you* need help?"

She looks at her shoes. "Because I've been feeling over the last few years like I've been disappearing, like I couldn't handle anything or anyone. It was like things was getting too hard to handle."

"You mean me?" I ask.

She shakes her head. "You were just a part of it. As soon as I left you here, it kind of woke me up. I went and found someone who can help me, you know, cope better, and that's why I'm here. "

That kinda surprises me. "You mean like a counselor or something?"

She nods. I can't picture her doing them sessions, but looking at Mama, she seem like she really trying and that she really do want me back. "Cole, I know you know what it feels like to be helpless, even if you don't say it. That's what I was feeling."

Helpless. I think of all the times I felt that way. Most of the time maybe. I thought I was the only one feeling like that. And there she was, feeling the same thing all along.

Man.

For most of my life, Mama was the only one who stood by me. The only one who raised me. The only one who tried. And what was I doin'? Skipping school and causing trouble and not pulling my own weight. I didn't have her back or protect her from the bad that's out there, 'cause I was just thinkin' of myself the whole time.

I wasn't living the Cowboy Way.

I feel my eyes get wet. Her eyes get all big like she's reading my mind. Soon tears is coming down her face and I gotta do everything I can not to cry too.

She takes a step closer to me and puts her hand softly on my arm. "Maybe we can be there for each other again," she whispers. "Like in the old days, remember? You and me. Then we both won't feel helpless no more."

I nod, feel my cheek is wet, and wipe it with my

sleeve. Harp abandoned me, but he trying to do better. Now I see Mama trying too. "Mama."

I fall into her arms. She holds me tight. We stand that way for the longest time.

After what seem like twenty minutes, she still silent like she don't wanna ruin the moment. She wipes her tears and tries to smile. I try too.

"You like it here, huh?" she asks.

I nod. "I'm gettin' used to it."

She takes a deep breath. "Well . . . maybe we could come to some kind of arrangement. . . ."

"Like what?" I ask.

"Like maybe you can live with me in the school year, then come back here next summer. Maybe having a break will help us both."

I look up at her, and I think about our place back home, the neighborhood I grew up in. I wonder if I'd fall back into my old ways or if the cowboy in me would keep me in line. I used to think there was no point in trying before, but now I can see things can change if you put your mind to it.

"You think I can still get into summer school?"

She takes my hand. "I already talked to your principal, and there's a space for you. He knows we been dealing with some personal problems. He reminded me that we really have to commit to working on this together. That might mean you working with a tutor and checking in with a truancy officer. But if you finish summer school, then he'll consider having you back without repeating. He's willing to give you another chance."

Just thinking about all that work makes me tired. But then I think about this past week and how all that hard work turned into something good.

She squeezes my hand. "I'm not saying it'll be easy, Cole. You have to put in the work and be part of the solution, not the problem." She takes my hand. "I'm just saying we should try again. Don't you think we deserve a second chance?"

I nod. But just when I think this can't get any weirder, Harper walks back in.

He sees us standing there, his eyes moving back and forth between us. He has this look on his face, relieved that she here and at the same time protective of me. It's a weird feeling after feeling for so long that nobody wanted me. Now we all standing here, looking at each other, not sure what to do next.

And I think, *This is the first time my family been all together since I was born.*

EPILOGUE

It's a year later, and me and Harp is staring each other down. Boo and Lightning doing the same thing, even trying to nip each other.

"You're not gonna hate me when I whup you, right?" Harp says.

I give him a look. "Old man, you been retired from this racetrack for almost a year. You don't think I can take you?"

He laughs. "It *is* your first race. Even *I* lost my first race."

I grin. "Don't you know you talking to a playa now?"

He nods. "Just because you made it through the school year without repeating don't mean you're a player. Just means you listened to me and your mama and put in the work. That's a start."

I nod toward Jamaica Bob. "Bob says I'm gonna give you a run for your money. We been practicing behind your back when you was at work."

"Yeah, I know. I also know Bob's dreads been sucking out his brain cells."

Big Dee breaks in. "Are you girls gonna gab all day or honor the Speedway with your presence?" He standing there with a red bandana in his hand, ready to get things started.

I shrug. "I just don't want Harp to die from a heart attack when he see how fast Boo go now."

The guys all bust up, Bob and Tex bumping fists. Nobody's laying bets on this, 'cept what you call a gentleman's bet, which means no cash. But that don't keep Tex from yelling, "I got my money on the boy!"

Harper can't believe it. "After all I done for him," he says, laughing. "Looks like they glad to have you back for the summer, Train."

I look over at the guys who is cheering me on, chanting, "Bring on the Train!"

Mama's standing on the sidelines, looking worried.

She got a smile on, but I know she thinks I'm gonna kill myself now that I'm startin' to race. She didn't want me racing, but that was part of the deal: summers with Harper, and that includes the Speedway. She wasn't supposed to come back till August, but she's already here a few weeks after she dropped me off, just to visit. Truth is, she misses me.

I wave at her, then I hear it: "Mama's boy!" Smush and Snapper crack up. I don't mind. It's just good to be back with Boo.

"Ready?" shouts Dee.

Ready as I'm gonna be.

"Set?"

Nothing's set. Harp's still fighting for the land with the City, trying to get them to sell. He slowly wearing them down and working double shifts exercising horses back at Philadelphia Park to save money for a down payment.

"Go!"

Boo takes a step, then I yell in his ear, "Boo!"

He takes off, and I can barely hold on. The wind sails by me, making my eyes water. Boo's running like he don't have a care in the world, like this is what he was made for. But I hear hoofs coming up fast behind us.

I don't know what's going to happen with me or Boo, but right now, the sun is shining and the wind is blowing away all my troubles. I look at the ground speeding by and think this is what it feels like to fly.

The stables is still alive for now, and so am I.

I'm barely holding on, but I'm holding on.

I see the finish line ahead, and I'm moving toward it. And that's all that matters.

AUTHOR'S NOTE

Though this story is fiction, it's inspired by the real-life urban black horsemen of North Philadelphia and the Brooklyn-Queens area. The picture here is from the *Life* magazine article that made me sit up and take notice, and led me to look deeper into this unique world.

The New York guys run the Federation of Black Cowboys, while the folks on Fletcher Street in Philly continue their battles against the City. Both use horses to keep young men off the streets. Both fight to maintain a tradition that has gone on for generations. But they're doing it their way, the Cowboy Way. More power to 'em.

To find out more about them, and to see videos and articles on these places, visit gregneri.com/cowboy.html.

LIFE

AMERICA'S WEEKEND M

STREET RIDERS

An unlikely tale of a tough Philadelphia
neighborhood and the
young horsemen who live there

Dante, 9,
with Slick
the pony

The Strange World of Collectibles ★ Easy Closet Makeovers

WEEKEND OF APRIL **22** 2005

ACKNOWLEDGMENTS

This is one of those books that I tinkered with for years before figuring out how to truly crack it. But I couldn't have done it without the following folks, so thanks to:

Doug Ertman, who sent me a *Life* magazine article about the Philly crew many years ago and said, "Here's your next book." I didn't believe him at the time, but what do I know?

My critique groups, who helped turn me into the writer I am, for reading my many different attempts over the years and quietly steering me in the right direction.

Jennifer Fox, my editor on *Chess Rumble* and *Yummy,* for her kindness and gracious support on this project.

Gail Ruffu, cousin and one of the unheralded advocates for horse rights in the racing world, for reading an early draft to make sure it would pass muster with people who know a thing or two about horses.

Martha Camarillo, whose amazing photography book *Fletcher Street* captures the real spirit of that community and confirmed for me there was a great story to be told here for teens.

The countless writers and videographers who have highlighted the black urban cowboy experience all over the U.S., and groups like the Federation of Black Cowboys for spreading the word by helping to get kids into horses instead of guns.

Ellis and the horsemen of Fletcher Street for really caring about these kids and the community. Long may you ride.

Michelle Shuman, tireless champion of the Fletcher Street guys, for her steady stream of e-mails, confirming rumors and thoughts, and for introducing me to Ellis and his posse down there while standing out in the cold rain as I asked questions.

Edward Necarsulmer IV, my main man. For his endless support and enthusiasm, and love of Dylan—thank you. I couldn't ask for a better agent.

Jesse Joshua Watson, collaborator in books and old-school hustle. My posse wouldn't be complete without him. Can't wait to hit the trail again, bro.

Andrea Tompa, my editor, who really fought for this book and made me feel like a writer of worth. You deserve a gold star for this one.

And finally, thanks to my family, who make it possible for me to even be a writer. I couldn't survive without them.